CHARLES E JACKSON II

Rhythm and Resolve

Finding My Voice

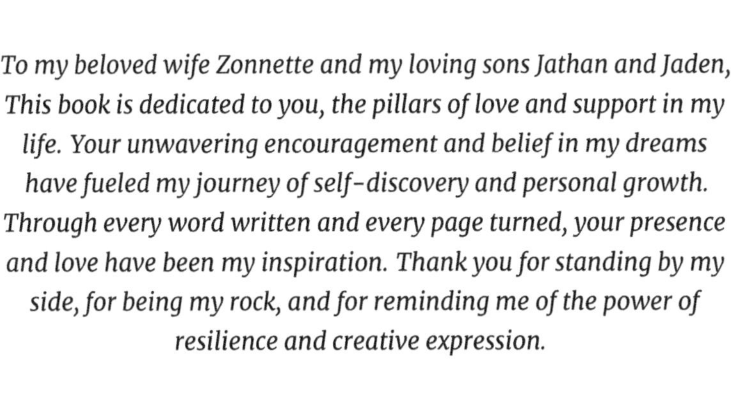

To my beloved wife Zonnette and my loving sons Jathan and Jaden,
This book is dedicated to you, the pillars of love and support in my
life. Your unwavering encouragement and belief in my dreams
have fueled my journey of self-discovery and personal growth.
Through every word written and every page turned, your presence
and love have been my inspiration. Thank you for standing by my
side, for being my rock, and for reminding me of the power of
resilience and creative expression.

Contents

Chapter 1: Doubts and Dissonance

The alarm blared through Malik's bedroom, jolting him awake. He groaned and slapped at the snooze button, but there was no escaping the reality of another school day. As he dragged himself out of bed, made his way to the bathroom, stared at himself in the mirror, the weight of his struggles settled on his shoulders like a heavy cloak. At 16 years old, he felt a constant struggle within himself, battling against a sense of self-worth and identity that seemed elusive. It wasn't just the challenges he faced as a teenager; it was a deeper battle that waged within his own mind and heart.

The doubts, the nagging feeling of not being good enough—it all seemed to linger in the shadows of his mind. A natural born leader - a fact he was yet to discover - Malik compared himself to other kids and often took the role of follower. He vacillated between feelings of love and acceptance and loneliness and dejection.

The dynamics of Malik's relationships played a significant role in shaping his self-perception. His family, although loving, had their own set of struggles. His parents, at times, overwhelmed with their own lives and responsibilities, seemed distant, leaving Malik craving a sense of connection and validation. While there was no denying their love for him, he yearned for a deep understanding and acceptance that would help him navigate the complexities of his teenage years.

   "Here we go again", he said to himself has he put the final touches on his outfit and left his room.

Malik trudged downstairs, the scent of coffee wafting through the air as his dad prepared for work. Dad, a former Marine, had always been the embodiment of discipline and strength. As Malik entered the kitchen, Dad's stern gaze met his tired eyes.

"Morning, son," Dad greeted, his voice laced with a mixture of concern and expectation. "You know, you've got to get it together. If you start the day expecting it to be a a drag, guess what, it will be! "Life is going to be tough at times," he continued, "but your perspective changes everything. Now stop dragging. If you miss the bus, you're walking. Your choice."

Malik nodded, the weight of his father's words sinking in. He understood Dad's intentions, but sometimes it felt as though the world demanded more from him than he could give. His parents, especially his dad, instilled in him a sense of discipline, integrity, and hard work.

While his father's strictness sometimes felt suffocating and annoyed Malik, he knew deep down that his dad's intentions were rooted in a desire to see him succeed, and to him that meant being a man of good character, having grit, and being resilient. However, the pressure to live up to his father's expectations often left Malik feeling overwhelmed and unsure of his own abilities.

His mind wandered to the lyrics he had scribbled in his notebook the previous night—a release, a form of self-expression that always brought him a solace escape.

"Sure, Dad," Malik replied, his voice heavy with resignation. He poured himself a bowl of cereal and glanced at the clock. The bus would be arriving soon, yet his heart felt heavy with the knowledge that another day of judgment and struggle awaited him.

As he stepped outside, he noticed his mom tending to her garden, her hands moving with purpose and care. Her bright smile greeted him, her Jamaican accent adding warmth to the morning air.

"Good morning, my love," Mom said, placing a hand on Malik's shoulder. "Remember, you have the power to overcome any challenge that comes your way today. Believe in yourself."

Compared to his dad, Malik's mother was his guiding light, always radiating love and support. She recognized Malik's unique talents and encouraged him to explore his passions. With her nurturing spirit, she created a safe space for him to express himself freely and discover his own voice. She listened when no one else would. When everyone else gave up on him, she never stop believing in him.

Malik nodded, appreciating his mom's unwavering support. He

took a deep breath, drawing strength from her words, before making his way to the bus stop.

Dressed in a casual yet fashionable ensemble, Malik catches the eye of passersby with his distinctive sense of style. He wore a graphic t-shirt that featured a collage of legendary hip-hop artist. The shirt perfectly complements his urban vibe, with its vibrant colors and intricate details.

His jeans have a comfortable yet trendy cut. The denim is adorned with subtle distressing and urban-inspired embellishments, adding a touch of edginess to his overall look.

As Malik strides confidently towards the bus stop, heads phones on and music thumping, all eyes are drawn to his prized possession — a fresh pair of red and black Air Jordan, limited first edition. The sneakers, meticulously selected to complete his ensemble, boast a sleek design and undeniable street appeal. Their classic silhouette and iconic Jumpman logo make a bold statement, reflecting Malik's love for both fashion and basketball culture.

A defining feature of Malik's appearance is his dreadlocks, a natural and striking expression of his personal identity. The thick, intertwined locks cascade down his shoulders, commanding attention wherever he goes.

Malik continues to move through the bustling urban landscape, his appearance radiating confidence and individuality. Yet, that all seems to fade once he steps on the bus.

Among the sea of faces, he felt a sense of isolation, as if he were an outsider observing the world from a distance.

The bus ride was filled with the usual chaos and chatter, but Malik found a safe place in his thoughts. His mind drifted to the lyrics he had been crafting—a raw expression of his struggles, his dreams, and his hopes. He longed to share his words with someone who would understand, someone who saw beyond the surface and into the depths of his soul.

School was a maze of expectations and judgment, and Malik often found himself stumbling through its corridors. The day progressed with a series of disinterested teachers, classmates who barely noticed his presence, and the feeling that he was constantly falling short. He could feel the weight of their assumptions and stereotypes pressing down on him, threatening to suffocate his spirit.

Malik's school, Winston High, is a bustling hub of energy and opportunity, tucked away in the heart of their vibrant neighborhood. As he walks through its hallways, the air is filled with a palpable sense of curiosity, creativity, and the pursuit of knowledge.

The exterior of the school is adorned with colorful murals, reflecting the diverse community it serves. The entrance is framed by a tall archway, engraved with empowering quotes and the school's motto, "Unlocking Creativity, Shaping Futures." It serves as a constant reminder of the transformative potential that lies within the walls of Winston High.

Entering the school, Malik is greeted by a vibrant mosaic floor, depicting symbols of knowledge, unity, and the arts. The hallways are adorned with student artwork, showcasing a kaleidoscope of creativity and self-expression. Bulletin boards display motivational messages and upcoming events, igniting a sense of anticipation and excitement.

The classrooms at Winston High are dynamic and engaging, designed to foster collaboration and critical thinking. Colorful posters and educational displays adorn the walls, inspiring students to think outside the box and explore new ideas. Flexible seating arrangements allow for versatile learning environments, encouraging students to find their own unique style of engagement.

The school's courtyard is a lively gathering place, buzzing with conversations, laughter, and the occasional impromptu jam session or roasting session, depending on the day. Colorful benches and tables provide spaces for students to relax, collaborate, and exchange ideas. Lush greenery and vibrant flowers create an oasis of tranquility amidst the bustling energy of the school, offering a serene escape during breaks and lunchtime.

Despite the vibrant atmosphere and inclusive environment at Winston High, Malik often finds himself wrestling with a sense of isolation and uncertainty. Surrounded by a sea of students who seem to effortlessly blend in, Malik can't help but feel like an outsider. The hallways that buzz with energy and camaraderie can sometimes magnify his own feelings of not quite fitting in.

While the school's inclusive spirit promotes acceptance, Malik's inner struggles persist. He questions his place within the social fabric of Winston High, unsure of where he truly belongs. The moments of self-doubt creep in, making him question his own worth.

At times, Malik's uncertainty seeps into his interactions with others. He second-guesses his words and actions, desperately yearning for acceptance and validation. The pressure to conform to societal norms can be overwhelming, leaving him feeling like he must sacrifice his authenticity to fit in.

During lunch, as Malik sat alone at his usual table, he pulled out his notebook and began to write. The words flowed effort-lessly, an outpouring of emotion onto the page. He poured his frustrations and aspirations into the lyrics, giving voice to the thoughts he had kept hidden for so long.

Lost in his own world, Malik didn't notice Travis, his childhood friend and skilled beat maker, approach the table. Travis peered over Malik's shoulder, catching a glimpse of the words on the page.

"Yo, Malik my guy, whatcha writing there?" Travis asked, his curiosity piqued.

Startled, Malik quickly closed his notebook, his cheeks flushing with embarrassment. "Uh, nothing, just some stuff."

Travis grinned mischievously. "Come on, man, you know you can trust me. We've been through it all together."

Reluctantly, Malik handed the notebook to Travis, his heart pounding in his chest. Travis skimmed through the lyrics, his eyes widening with each word. He looked up at Malik, his face lit up with excitement.

"Malik, this is fire! These lyrics... they're powerful, real," Travis exclaimed, a surge of energy coursing through his veins. "You've got talent, man. Let's work on this together, make it come alive with a fire beat."

Malik stared at Travis, a mix of disbelief and hope bubbling within him. He had always admired Travis's skills mixing music, and now, his friend was offering to collaborate, to bring Malik's words to life. It was a glimmer of validation, a spark of possibility in a world that often felt suffocating.

With a nod and a grateful smile, Malik knew that this moment was the beginning of something transformative. The shadows of self-doubt that had haunted him for so long were slowly fading, replaced by a newfound determination to find his voice and embrace his passion for music.

"Young men, you should already be in class," a booming voice echoed across the bustling courtyard, pulling Malik and Travis from their engrossing conversation. It was Ms. Jackson, the formidable principal of the school, making her presence known. With her sharp gaze and no-nonsense demeanor, she had earned a reputation as the disciplinarian in Malik's life. Their encounters were often characterized by tension and clashes of wills. Ms. Jackson seemed to only see Malik through the lens of his academic setbacks and disruptive behavior, which only fueled his frustration and resistance.

Reluctantly tearing himself away from Travis, Malik nodded and mumbled a quick goodbye. "Later, bro," Travis replied with a nod and a knowing smile. They had shared countless conversations and creative brainstorming sessions, forging a bond built on their shared love for music and their mutual dreams of making an impact through their art.

With a heavy sigh, Malik locked eyes with Ms. Jackson, her stern expression leaving no room for defiance. He grabbed his worn notebook and slung his bag over his shoulder, mustering a hint of rebelliousness in his stride as he made his way to 5th period—the class he somewhat enjoyed.

As the final school bell chimed, releasing students from the confines of their academic responsibilities, Malik and Travis huddled together, their voices a harmonious blend of excitement and determination. The world outside faded into the background as they passionately exchanged ideas, sharing their visions and ambitions. A sense of purpose began to bloom within Malik's heart, fueled by the belief that he had something important to say, a message that needed to be heard.

In that moment, surrounded by the camaraderie of a like-minded friend and the stirring melodies of their shared dreams, Malik's doubts and frustrations began to dissipate. He felt the weight of Ms. Jackson's judgment and the pressure of expectations slowly lifting off his shoulders. The power of his voice, the potential of his artistry, became clear.

After bidding Travis farewell, Malik found himself drawn to the top row of the bleachers overlooking the football field. The sound of whistles and the thud of bodies colliding filled the air as the team below engaged in intense practice drills. It was a scene of discipline, focus, and teamwork—a stark contrast to Malik's own struggles to find his place and purpose.

Sitting alone in the solitude of the bleachers, Malik opened his worn notebook, its pages filled with scribbled verses, raw emotions, and the fragments of ideas that had been brewing within him. With pen in hand, he immersed himself in the act of writing, the world around him fading into the background. Words flowed from his pen like a symphony of thoughts, each line carrying a piece of his soul.

As the sun dipped below the horizon, casting hues of orange and purple across the sky, Malik's thoughts danced between the lines of his notebook. He poured his heart onto the pages, navigating the maze of his emotions and experiences. Each stroke of the pen was a step closer to untangling the complexities within him, revealing the truth and authenticity he longed to express.

In the distance, the football team's chants and cheers echoed, serving as a reminder of the unity and collective spirit they embodied. Malik couldn't help but feel a sense of envy for their camaraderie, their clear sense of purpose on the field. But deep down, he knew his purpose lay beyond the confines of the football field. It resided in the lyrics and beats that flowed through his veins, in the power of his voice to ignite change and inspire others.

As he sat there, enveloped in the stillness of the evening, he realized that his journey to finding his voice would be a symphony of self-discovery, a harmonious blend of introspection, passion, and perseverance.

Dad's familiar car pulled into the parking lot, its headlights cutting through the gathering darkness. Malik closed his notebook, tucking it safely into his backpack, his words etched into his heart. With a renewed sense of purpose, he descended the bleachers, his steps light but resolute.

As he approached the car, Malik could feel the presence of his dad's unwavering support, a silent understanding passing between them. There was a mutual recognition that Malik was on a transformative journey as he navigated his teenage years and time at Winston High. One that would test his resilience and push him to his limits. But in that moment, as he slid into the passenger seat, a small smile graced his lips. He knew he wasn't alone anymore. The rhythm and resolve within him had found a partner in his dad's unwavering belief in him.

As the car pulled away from the school, the football field disappeared into the rearview mirror. Malik glanced at his reflection, his eyes shining with determination and a fresh sense of purpose. He knew that what he was cooking up with Travis was just the beginning—the prelude to a symphony of self-discovery, creativity, and the unyielding pursuit of his dreams.

In the fading light of the day, Malik clutched his notebook tightly, feeling the weight of his lyrics and dreams intertwine. The journey ahead would be filled with challenges, but for the first time in a long while, Malik felt a glimmer of hope—a rhythm and resolve that would guide him toward finding his voice.

Chapter 2: Shadows in the Classroom

School had always been a battlefield for Malik, where he fought against his own academic shortcomings and the stigma that came with it. Despite his parents' high expectations and the relentless pressure to excel, Malik found himself struggling to keep up with his peers. His grades were consistently mediocre, and he often found himself getting into trouble for his disruptive behavior.

Among other kids at school, he often felt like an outsider. He was caught between the pressures of fitting in and the longing to be true to himself. The fear of judgment and rejection gnawed at him, leading him to compromise his authenticity at times. He longed for friends who would accept him unconditionally, supporting him in his pursuit of self-discovery.

Every day, Malik would sit in class, feeling lost and disconnected. The material seemed to go over his head, and he found it difficult to concentrate on the lessons being taught. He would stare at the blackboard, the words blurring together into a meaningless jumble. The more he tried to grasp the concepts, the more they seemed to slip away.

Teachers labeled him as a lost cause, dismissing him as unmotivated and lacking in intelligence. They couldn't see the potential hidden beneath his struggles. Malik's constant academic setbacks took a toll on his self-esteem. He questioned his own intelligence and worthiness, wondering if he was destined to be a failure.

Classmates, too, began to form their own opinions, viewing him as nothing more than a troublemaker. Their disapproving glances and mocking whispers only fueled his feelings of alienation. Malik felt like an outsider, constantly at odds with the expectations of his peers and society. He yearned for acceptance and understanding, but it always seemed just out of reach.

The pressure to succeed weighed heavily on Malik's shoulders. It seemed as though everyone around him had lofty expectations for his academic performance. His parents, in particular, held high standards, hoping to see him excel and secure a bright future. While they meant well, their constant push for success sometimes felt suffocating.

In the midst of this challenging environment, Malik's behavior began to reflect his frustrations. Frustration turned into rebellion, and he found himself engaging in acts of defiance and disrupting the classroom. The attention he received from his misbehavior only deepened the negative perception others had of him.

Yet, beneath the surface of his academic struggles, Malik possessed a natural curiosity and a hunger for knowledge. Outside of the confines of the classroom, he sought relief in books and documentaries, immersing himself in subjects that fascinated him. He found joy in learning about topics that aligned with his passions, such as music, history, and social issues.

Despite the difficulties he faced, there were a few teachers who recognized Malik's potential and refused to give up on him. They saw past his disruptive behavior and encouraged him to tap into his strengths. These mentors offered support and guidance, providing extra resources and engaging in one-on-one conversations to help him navigate his challenges.

Among these teachers was Ms. Bing, his compassionate 5th period English teacher who saw Malik's passion for storytelling and creative expression. Ms. Bing saw beyond his academic struggles and recognized his creative potential. She fostered an environment of inclusivity and encouraged Malik to embrace his unique perspective. She had a way of connecting with those who, like Malik, felt ostracized for being different.

One day, Malik left his notebook open as he left his seat. Ms. Bing noticed the writings and asked to take a look. Malik hesitated, then handed her the notebook; a sacred diary of his thoughts and feelings in lyrical form.

She read the same rap lyrics Malik had previously shared with Travis. Her response, the same. "Malik, this is some powerful and gripping poetry!" Malik didn't see himself as a poet, yet could not keep the corners of his lips from turning up as he smiled and blushed with relief.

Recognizing his talent, Ms. Bing encouraged Malik to explore writing and hip hop as an outlet for his thoughts and emotions. She assigned creative writing projects that allowed Malik to channel his energy and frustrations into imaginative stories and poems for her class that he could also use in his artistic expressions.

Ms. Bing's belief in Malik's potential sparked an even greater glimmer of hope within him. She gave him the confidence to express himself through writing, as she recognized the power of words to heal and transform. For the first time, Malik began to see himself as more than just a troubled student. He started to envision a future where his creativity and unique perspective could be celebrated, rather than suppressed.

After leaving the pressures and stresses of school behind, Malik found consolation in the moments when he could escape the confines of the classroom, retreat to his room, grab his headphones and shed the weight of the world by losing himself in the beats of his favorite artists.

As he pushed open the door to his room, a wave of familiarity and comfort washed over him. The space, a reflection of his evolving identity and passions, was a testament to his teenage years.

His eyes were immediately drawn to the vibrant sneaker collection that lined the walls, each pair meticulously arranged and proudly displayed. The colorful array of Air Jordans, or Nike Dunks told a story of Malik's love for street fashion and his ever-growing sense of style. The sneakers seemed to come alive, each pair possessing its own personality and history, imbued with the memories of countless walks and dances to the beat of Malik's favorite tunes.

In the corner of the room, an electric drum set from his middle school days sat collecting dust. Its once-shining cymbals and drum pads had been witness to Malik's early forays into rhythm and beats. Although he hadn't played them in a while, the drums remained a reminder of his musical journey, a symbol of his innate creativity and the potential that lay within him. The faint echo of the drumbeats still resonated in the air, a reminder of the dreams that awaited their realization.

A bean bag chair, well-worn and molded to fit Malik's contours, beckoned him with its inviting embrace. It was the throne of relaxation, a place where he could sink into its softness and lose himself in a sea of melodies and lyrics. The chair had become a trusted companion, witnessing countless moments of introspection, as Malik would sit for hours, headphones on, immersing himself in the sounds that fueled his artistic passion.

The walls of his room were adorned with a collage of posters, a visual tapestry of Malik's eclectic tastes and influences. Music legends like Tupac, Biggie, and Jay-Z gazed down upon him, their timeless expressions etched into the fabric of his creative psyche. Posters of influential artists adorned the spaces in between, representing the diverse genres that inspired and shaped his musical aspirations. The room seemed to vibrate with the energy of these icons, their presence lending an air of inspiration and motivation.

On his desk, stacks of books and music magazines stood as

testaments to Malik's thirst for knowledge and artistic exploration. Novels, biographies, and poetry collections formed a literary landscape that fueled his imagination and broadened his perspectives. Music magazines provided a window into the ever-evolving world of hip hop and offered insights into the lives and creative processes of his favorite artists. The desk, cluttered yet organized, served as the epicenter of Malik's creative endeavors, a place where ideas were born and dreams took shape.

Proudly displayed on one wall, a collection of basketball jerseys told the story of Malik's love for the game. Each jersey represented a different team and player, a homage to the basketball legends who had graced the courts and inspired him to strive for greatness. The jerseys were more than just fabric and colors; they embodied the spirit of competition, teamwork, and the pursuit of excellence that Malik admired.

As Malik soaked in the sights and sounds of his room, he felt a sense of calm wash over him. This space, filled with mementos of his journey, offered him a sanctuary from the outside world. It was here that he could embrace his true self, free from the judgments and expectations of others. In this room, surrounded by the tangible reminders of his passions and interests, Malik felt a deep sense of belonging and authenticity.

His room was more than just four walls and a ceiling; it was a reflection of his evolving identity, a space where dreams took flight and possibilities were limitless. It was a sanctuary where Malik could retreat, recharge, and reaffirm his sense of self. In the comfort of his own personal haven, he was reminded of his own potential, and he knew that no matter the challenges he faced outside those walls, he could always find safety, inspiration, and a resounding sense of belonging within the confines of his room.

It was during these times that he was discovering and embracing his true passion—music.

Chapter 3: The Beat Within

midst the twilight of that evening, as the sun painted the sky with hues of orange and purple, Malik and his mom sat on the porch, their voices mingling with the gentle breeze. The rhythmic lilt of her Jamaican accent, which she often dipped into, added a melodic cadence to their conversation, infusing their exchange with warmth and cultural richness.

With all the craziness and the turmoil of his teenage years, his mom was one constant source of support and encouragement for Malik—Shining with love and pride, she had always been his biggest fan, firmly believing in his abilities and potential.

Growing up in Jamaica, she had a deep-rooted love for music herself, and she understood the power it held to uplift and inspire. Malik's mom would often share stories of her own experiences with music, recounting the vibrant rhythms of reggae and the profound lyrics that spoke to the soul. Her love for music became contagious, igniting a flame within Malik's heart.

"Mom, remember when you used to tell me stories about growing up in Jamaica?" Malik asked, a twinkle in his eyes.

His mom smiled, her face illuminated by the soft glow of the porch light. "Oh, yes! I used to share so many stories with you, Malik," she replied, her voice brimming with nostalgia. "I wanted you to know where I came from, our roots, and the music that runs through our veins."

Malik leaned in, captivated by her words. "Tell me again about the dances and the music you would listen to," he urged, his curiosity shining through.

His mom's eyes sparkled as she recalled those vibrant memories. "In Jamaica, we had our own language of music, my son. We would sway to the infectious rhythms of reggae, our bodies moving to the beat as if possessed by the spirit of the music. The sounds of Bob Marley's 'One Love' would fill the air, and we would sing along with passion, letting the music wash over us and transport us to a place of unity and love."

Malik nodded, absorbing every word. "And the dances? The ones you used to tell me about?" he pressed further.

A mischievous smile danced on his mom's lips. "Ah, the dances! We would gather in the open-air dancehalls, our bodies pulsating to the energetic sounds of ska and reggae music. The bass would reverberate through the night, and we would move with freedom and abandon, releasing all worries and troubles through the power of dance."

As they reminisced, their conversation shifted to the present, with Malik sharing his latest rap compositions and pouring his heart into the lyrics. His mom listened intently, her eyes filled with pride and admiration. She offered gentle guidance, occasionally slipping into Patois, the native language of her Jamaican roots, to express her appreciation for his words.

"Malik, mi luv ow yuh express yuhself pan di rhythm," his mom exclaimed, her voice filled with genuine excitement. "Yuh ave di fire and di passion. Yuh words dem hit di heart, just like how Bob Marley and Buju Banton did back inna mi time."

Malik grinned, the praise from his mom fueling his creative fire. He felt a sense of validation and belonging as he shared this deep connection with her, one that transcended generations and geography. The bond between Malik and his mom grew stronger as they shared their mutual love for music.

Their conversation carried on, their voices blending harmoniously with the sounds of nature surrounding them. The music that had shaped his mom's upbringing now resonated within Malik's soul, intertwining their stories and forging an unbreakable bond. Malik felt a deep connection with his Jamaican roots, as he embraced the cultural influences and begin to see how it shaped his identity and could shape his music.

Malik felt inspired to head to his favorite writing spot, the neighborhood park. With his mom's love and support echoing in his heart, he embarked on a journey of self-expression, armed with the melodies of his Jamaican heritage and the wisdom imparted by his mom.

The sun dipped below the horizon as Malik walked down the street, his steps in sync with the rhythmic beats pulsing through his earphones. The melodic sounds of his favorite hip-hop tracks provided a soundtrack to his thoughts, inspiring his creativity and pushing him to explore the depths of his own talent.

As he approached the neighborhood park, a vibrant tapestry of sights and sounds unfolded before Malik's eyes. The park was a lively gathering place, brimming with energy and activity. The warm glow of a distant streetlamp cast a gentle illumination, creating a serene ambiance.

In one corner of the park, Malik spotted a group of friends engaged in a spirited pick-up game of basketball. The rhythmic thud of sneakers on the pavement echoed through the air as players dribbled and leaped, their competitive spirit fueling their every move. Cheers and playful banter filled the space, creating a lively atmosphere that drew Malik's attention.

Not far from the basketball court, a skate park came alive with the sounds of wheels rolling, grinding, and sliding against concrete. Skateboarders of all skill levels glided with grace and confidence, executing daring tricks and gravity-defying flips. The air was filled with a mix of exhilaration and camaraderie as skaters encouraged and cheered one another on.

As Malik made his way further into the park, he noticed a diverse array of individuals engaged in various forms of exercise. Joggers gracefully weaved through pathways, their rhythmic footsteps creating a harmonious symphony with the surrounding nature. Groups of friends gathered for outdoor yoga sessions, finding peace and serenity amidst the tranquil surroundings. Fitness enthusiasts engaged in calisthenics and circuit training, their bodies moving in synchrony with their determination and dedication.

Absorbing the lively scenes unfolding around him, Malik couldn't help but feel a sense of belonging. The park was more than just a physical space; it was a symbol of connection, a testament to the power of shared experiences and the unity found in diverse passions. In this vibrant tapestry of life, Malik found inspiration and a reminder that within the park's embrace, dreams could be nurtured, talents could be honed, and connections could be forged.

Amidst the activity, a figure caught Malik's attention. Travis, his childhood friend and beat maker extraordinaire, sat on a weathered bench, his fingers expertly tapping on a beat-up drum pad. The rhythmic beats flowed effortlessly from his fingertips, filling the air with a captivating melody. Passersby paused, drawn to the hypnotic rhythm, their heads nodding and bodies swaying in sync with the music.

Malik took a deep breath, letting the sights and sounds of the park fill his soul. The beat of Travis's drum pad blended harmoniously with the laughter, cheers, and whispers of the park's inhabitants. It was a symphony of life, an affirmation that within this community, his voice and his music would find a place to thrive.

Malik quickened his pace, anticipation tingling in his veins.

"Travis! What are you doing here?"

Travis grinned, his eyes sparkling with excitement. "Malik, what up my guy! I've been working on some beats, trying to find that perfect sound for you as I said. Thought I'd come here, where the rhythm of our neighborhood can inspire me."

Malik nodded, a surge of adrenaline coursing through his body. "You know, I've been working on some lyrics too. Can I show you?"

Travis's smile widened. "Absolutely, bro! Lay it on me."

As they settled on the park bench, Malik opened his notebook, carefully turning the pages to reveal his heartfelt lyrics.

"I am a mosaic of scars, each telling a tale,
    I wear them proudly, they shall not make me frail.
    For I am the artistry of my own creation,
    A masterpiece in progress, in constant transformation.

Through words that flow like rivers in my veins,
    I break free from the shackles, release these chains.
    I dance with vulnerability, bask in authenticity,
    Embracing imperfections, I unlock my identity......"

The words flowed effortlessly from his lips, a river of emotions blending seamlessly with Travis's beats. The air crackled with creative energy as they found a harmonious connection, the music breathing life into Malik's words.

Travis's head bobbed to the rhythm, his eyes locked on Malik. His words floated in the air like poetry in motion. As if drawn by an invisible force, curious onlookers began to gather around, their eyes widening with anticipation.

The kids playing ball, with their wide-eyed wonder, were the first to be captivated by Malik's words. They formed a small circle, their faces filled with awe and excitement. They whispered among themselves, oohing and ahhing at the heartfelt lines that spilled effortlessly from Malik's lips.

Word spread quickly, and soon, other park-goers couldn't resist the magnetic pull of Malik's lyrical prowess. They paused in their activities, their curiosity piqued by the infectious energy emanating from the impromptu gathering. The skate park emptied momentarily as skaters set aside their boards to join the growing audience.

As the lyrics flowed, the crowd became immersed in Malik's storytelling. The rhythm of his words resonated with their hearts, inviting them on a journey of emotions and experiences. Heads nodded in time with the Travis's beat, bodies swayed with the melodies woven into each of Malik's lyrics.

Travis, grinning from ear to ear, watched the growing crowd with pride. He knew firsthand the power of Malik's music and the impact it would have on those who listened. As the kids and adults alike hung on every word, Travis couldn't help but feel a sense of fulfillment knowing that he had played a part in bringing this moment to life.

Encouraged by the enthusiastic response, Malik's voice grew stronger, he stood on the park bench, his delivery more passionate. He poured his heart and soul into each line, connecting with the audience on a deep, emotional level. Applause and cheers erupted between bars, an acknowledgment of the raw talent and vulnerability that Malik shared so effortlessly.

In that park, under the open sky and amidst the collective energy of the crowd, something magical happened. Strangers became united, connected by the universal language of music. The oohs and ahhs turned into laughter and shared appreciation as the performance reached its crescendo.

As Malik finished his last line, the park erupted in a wave of applause and genuine admiration. The gathering of onlookers, now transformed into a community of supporters, expressed their gratitude for the heartfelt performance. They knew they had witnessed something special—a moment of pure authenticity and artistic expression.

For Malik, the gathering was more than just applause; it was validation. In the faces of those who listened, he saw reflection, inspiration, and a shared understanding of the power of music to bridge divides and touch souls.

As the crowd dispersed, each person carried a piece of Malik's music with them, their hearts stirred by the melodies and lyrics that had woven their way into their consciousness.

"Malik, no cap my guy, that was incredible! Your words... they have power, they have meaning," Travis exclaimed, his voice filled with awe. "You saw what just happened. We've got something special here."

"And I ain't just saying that because I made the beat." They both laughed. "Let's make magic!"

Malik's heart swelled with pride and a stirring sense of purpose that he hadn't felt before. Collaborating with Travis had unlocked a wellspring of confidence within him. He realized that his love for music went beyond a mere passion—it was his avenue for self-expression, a tool to navigate the complexities of his identity.

Days turned into weeks, and Malik and Travis dedicated themselves to perfecting their craft. They would often meet at the park, bringing their collective talents to the forefront. Malik's lyrics poured forth, a tapestry of emotions and experiences, while Travis's beats became the heartbeat of their musical partnership.

One afternoon, Malik's girlfriend, Mariah, joined them at the park, her radiant smile lighting up the surroundings. She had always been a source of support and inspiration for Malik, her fashion-forward spirit a perfect complement to his artistic endeavors.

"Hey, guys! What's poppin'?" Mariah asked, settling onto the bench beside them.

Travis chuckled. "What's poppin is this track we're cooking up, Mariah. Malik here is spitting fire with his lyrics, and I'm adding the beats to bring them to life."

Curiosity danced in Mariah's eyes as she listened intently to the collaboration. The fusion of Malik's poetic verses and Travis's pulsating beats igniting her own creative spirit.

"Malik, this is amazing!" Mariah exclaimed, her voice filled with admiration. "Your lyrics are raw and powerful, and the way Travis weaves the beats around them—it's like a symphony. You both have something special here."

Malik's face flushed with gratitude. To have Mariah's unwavering support meant the world to him. He felt surrounded by a circle of friendship and artistic camaraderie that gave him the courage to dream beyond the constraints of his past.

As the weeks went by, Malik's musical journey began to weave its way into the fabric of his daily life. He found himself penning lyrics during free moments at school, capturing snippets of conversations, and the emotions that swirled within him. It was through his music that he discovered a newfound freedom—a voice that had been silenced for far too long.

One evening, as Malik sat on the porch, his notebook in hand, his grandma, who everyone affectionately called Ma, approached him. Ma held a special place in Malik's heart. They shared a bond that transcended generations and brought comfort to his restless soul. Her wisdom, patience, and unconditional love served as a guiding light in Malik's life. She saw the potential within him, constantly reminding him of his worth and encouraging him to embrace his unique identity, and when he felt alone, to remember that God was always there.

"Malik, my boy, I can see the fire burning within you," Ma said, her voice soft and reassuring. "Your music—it carries the beat of your soul. Embrace it fully and let it guide you."

Malik nodded, grateful for Ma's insight and guidance. Her words confirmed what he had felt deep within—his talents were a gift and his music was not just a creative outlet, but a force that connected him to his roots, to his family, and to something greater than himself.

With each passing day, Malik's confidence grew. He reveled in the knowledge that he had found his voice, a vessel for his thoughts, dreams, and the power of his own narrative. Through his collaboration with Travis, he had discovered the transformative potential of their music to touch the hearts of others.

As the sun dipped below the horizon once more, Malik closed his notebook, the melodies and lyrics engraved deep within his being. The journey had only just begun, but he knew with unwavering certainty that the beat within him was destined to create waves, inspiring others and weaving a tapestry of grit and self-expression.

Chapter 4: Lyrics Unveiled

The dimly lit basement served as Malik and Travis's sanctuary—a space where their creative energies could flow freely. The room was adorned with posters of their musical inspirations, their larger-than-life images serving as reminders of the heights they aspired to reach.

Malik paced back and forth, his mind abuzz with anticipation. He clutched his notebook, filled with a fresh batch of lyrics he had meticulously crafted over the past week. He couldn't wait to unveil his latest creations to Travis, eager to see how their collaboration would breathe life into his words.

Travis sat at his mixer, his fingers tapping out a rhythmic pattern on the drum pads. He looked up, a wide grin spreading across his face as Malik entered the makeshift booth.

"Malik, my man! I've been itching to hear what you've cooked up this time," Travis exclaimed, his eyes shining with excitement. "Let's hear it!"

Malik took a deep breath, gathering his thoughts. He flipped open his notebook, the pages filled with ink-stained verses that spoke of resilience, identity, and the power of self-expression. He cleared his throat and began to recite his lyrics with a fiery determination.

"Yeah, yo, check it out, listen up...
     From the shadows I rise, my spirit unbound,
     A voice in the chaos, a thunderous sound.
     Through the weight of my struggles, I find my own way,
     Unveiling my truth, no longer afraid.

So here you go, this rap is a reminder, let your true colors show.
     In a world of conformity, where they try to shape your mold,
     I'm here to tell you, dare to be bold.

They say, "Fit in, don't stand out, follow the crowd,"
     But I say, "Nah, that's not how we get down."
     It's time to break the chains, break the status quo,

Unleash your inner fire, let your true self glow.
     Dare to be different, embrace your uniqueness,
     Don't let them dim your light, don't let them weaken us.
     Stand tall, be proud, let your voice be heard,
     Break free from the chains, be the flock's black bird."

Travis's eyes widened, captivated by the raw emotion in Malik's voice.

"Malik, that's lit!" Travis exclaimed, his voice filled with admiration. "Your lyrics hit straight to the core, man. It's like you're speaking from the depths of your soul. I can already hear the beats in my head. Let's bring this to life!"

Malik's heart soared with validation. The unyielding support from Travis fueled his confidence, instilling in him the belief that his words carried power. Together, they dove into the creative process, seamlessly merging their talents to create a symphony of words and music.

Hours turned into days, and days into weeks, as Malik and Travis immersed themselves in their craft. They experimented with different melodies, incorporating those staple reggae rhythms, refining the beats and arrangements until they found the perfect harmony to complement Malik's lyrics. The late nights and early mornings were a testament to their shared dedication and passion.

Inspired by the rhythm and poetry of hip hop, Malik began to explore his own abilities as a wordsmith. He delved into the art of writing rap lyrics, immersing himself in the intricacies of rhyme schemes and storytelling. It was through the act of writing that Malik found an outlet for his emotions, a canvas on which he could paint the vivid picture of his experiences.

Late into the night, Malik would sit in his room, pen in hand, pouring his heart and soul onto the page. The words flowed from him effortlessly, each line revealing a piece of his innermost thoughts and desires. With every verse, he discovered a piece of himself, his struggles, his dreams, and his hopes for the future. It was through music that Malik started to discover his own voice and the power it held.

The more he immersed himself in the world of hip hop, the more he realized the profound impact it had on his life. He listened to the music of his favorite artists, studying their lyrics and dissecting the emotions they conveyed. It became a form of therapy, a means to make sense of the complexities of his own journey.

One evening, Malik received a call from Mariah. She had been following his musical journey closely, attending their impromptu jam sessions at the park whenever possible. Her voice bubbled with excitement as she shared some news.

"Malik, guess what? I've been talking to my cousin, Jason—he's a filmmaker," Mariah said, her voice brimming with enthusiasm. "He's working on a short film and is looking for original music. I immediately thought of you and Travis!"

Malik's heart leaped with anticipation. The prospect of their music being featured in a film was a dream come true. It was an opportunity to reach a wider audience, to share their message of resolve and self-expression.

"Wow, Mariah, that's amazing! We'd love to be a part of it," Malik replied, his voice filled with gratitude. "Tell Jason we're in!"

Invigorated, Malik and Travis worked tirelessly, pouring their hearts and souls into creating the perfect soundtrack for Jason's film. Ironically, it featured a lead character in foster care on a similar path of self discovery as Malik after an addiction caused her to hit rock bottom.

Each note, each lyric became a brushstroke on the canvas of their shared vision. The prospect of their music resonating with others fueled their drive to push the boundaries of their creative abilities.

As the final day of recording arrived, Malik, Travis, and Mariah made their way to the studio where Jason was putting the finishing touches on his film. The air buzzed with excitement as the team gathered around, ready to experience the fusion of visuals and music.

The lights dimmed, and the film began to play on the screen. The images danced, seamlessly blending with Malik and Travis's music. It was an immersive experience—a vivid tapestry of emotions woven together by their collaboration.

As the final scene faded to black, the room erupted into applause. Jason beamed with pride, his eyes glistening with gratitude.

"Malik, Travis, you guys have created something truly special," Jason said, his voice filled with admiration. "Your music has added a whole new layer of depth and meaning to this film. It's pure magic."

Malik's favorite scene was of the lead character Sadie, looking at her reflection in the window as she rode the metro. She saw past the surface of her pink highlights, nose and ear piercings, tattoos, and the heads phones she wore and immersed herself in the wave of emotions conjured up by the words of one of Malik's songs blasting in her ears:

"Looking in the mirror, it's time to let you know.
    This rap is dedicated to the reflection I see,

A journey of self-discovery, let's set it free.
    I gaze into the mirror, what do I see?
    A reflection of a warrior, powerful and free.

Eyes shining bright, like stars in the night,
    I embrace my flaws, I'm a beautiful sight.
    Every scar tells a story, each line has a tale,
    I'm a masterpiece in progress, destined to prevail.

I see strength in my eyes, determination in my soul,
    I'm on a path to greatness, that's my ultimate goal.
    In the mirror, I see resilience and grace,
    A spirit unbreakable, ready to face any chase.
    I'm not defined by society's standards or trends,
    I define my own worth, my spirit transcends."

Malik could relate to that moment. The moment you start to see yourself as more than a failure, more than an outcast, more than a mistake, more than someone unloved and unwanted, but rather someone unique, gifted, and created on purpose with purpose. Someone with so much to offer the world.

Those are the moments that define us, not our past. Malik could hear his dad saying,
    "We all make mistakes Malik, and if we let it, the past will hunt us. But learn from the past, don't live in it."

Malik's heart swelled with a mixture of joy and accomplishment.

To witness their music intertwine with the visuals, evoking emotions and leaving an indelible mark on the audience, was a testament to the power of their collaboration.

In that moment, Malik realized that their journey went beyond personal growth and creative fulfillment. Their music had the potential to touch lives, to inspire others to embrace their own unique voices and find joy and comfort in self-expression. To rise up out of despair and live!

As they left Jason's studio, Malik, Travis, and Mariah walked through the city streets, their steps light and purposeful. The path ahead was uncertain, but the trio shared an unbreakable bond, fueled by a shared passion for music and fashion and the belief that their voices and unique gifts could create ripples of positive change.

With each lyric unveiled, each beat carefully crafted, Malik's sense of self-worth grew stronger. He had discovered his voice, and he was determined to use it to inspire others—to lend courage to those who doubted themselves, and to shine a light on the identity crisis he and others like him were facing.

Chapter 5: Harmony of Struggles

The scent of jerk chicken filled the air as Malik stepped into the warm embrace of his home. The rhythmic melodies of reggae floated through the rooms, emanating from the speakers where his mom, dad, and Ma had gathered. The familiar beats and vibrant sounds were a testament to his Jamaican heritage, a reminder of the rich cultural tapestry that shaped his identity.

"Mom, I'm home!" Malik called out, his voice filled with affection.

Mom turned, her face radiant with joy. "Welcome, my love. Dinner will be ready soon. Sit and relax."

As Malik settled onto the couch, surrounded by the familiar sights and sounds of his Jamaican upbringing, he couldn't help but reflect on the impact his mom's culture had on his journey of self-discovery. Her unwavering support and spiritual wisdom had shaped his perspective, instilling in him a deep connection to his roots.

His mom joined him on the couch, her eyes filled with a mixture of pride and love. "Malik, my son, your music—it carries the heartbeat of our heritage infused with the joys and pains of your journey. Embrace it fully, and it will guide you and open doors for your message."

Malik smiled, his heart swelling with gratitude. "Thank you, Mom. Your belief in me means a lot."

Just then, Dad walked in, his presence commanding respect. "Son, your mom is right. Embrace your heritage, let the rhythm of your music weave the threads of your identity.

Malik's dad was very eclectic when it came to music. A talented musician himself, at any given moment you could find the two of them in the car vibing to his dad's favorite 90's or 2000's hip hop track. The bass from the 12" subs beating against Malik's back and reverberating through his chest as he sat on the passenger side watching his dad bob his head and flow. Other times, he would catch his dad sitting on the balcony with his mom, wine glass in hand, swaying back and forth to the sultry sounds of Neo-soul or a Country love ballad. There were not many genres dad would not listen to.

"Let everything you create be an out pouring and overflow of your own thoughts, experiences, and the things that consume you", he continued. "Embrace them, and you will remain true to yourself."

Malik nodded, acknowledging his dad, a wordsmith and wise man in his own right. Malik's mind filled with determination.

His parents words resonated deeply within him, reinforcing the importance of embracing all facets of his identity, including the cultural influences that had shaped him.

Days turned into weeks, and Malik's music continued to evolve. The bond between him and Travis grew stronger, their collaboration thriving as they refined their craft. Malik continued incorporating elements of reggae and dancehall into their compositions, honoring his Jamaican roots and infusing his music with his own unique flavor.

One evening, as Malik and Travis fine-tuned their latest track, Mariah entered the basement studio, her eyes filled with admiration as she listened to the fusion of melodies and lyrics.

"Wow, Bae, this sounds incredible! Your blend of hip-hop and reggae—it's a harmonious marriage," Mariah exclaimed, her voice filled with genuine excitement. "You're embracing all parts of yourself, and it's beautiful to witness."

Malik beamed at Mariah, grateful for her unwavering support. With her by his side, he felt invincible—a team ready to take on the world with his music and her fashion. Her presence served as a constant reminder that he was not alone in his journey of self-discovery.

As their music continued to evolve, Malik and Travis decided to showcase their talents at the local community center. The stage was set, the anticipation thick in the air as the audience gathered.

The room buzzed with energy as Malik stepped onto the stage, his heart pounding with a mixture of nervousness and excitement. Travis stood beside him, their partnership solidified by countless hours of hard work and shared dreams. Malik looked out across the crowd at all the familiar faces. J.R. was seated next to Ma while Dad stood in the back, arm crossed leaning against the wall. Also among the rowdy crowd was Ava Jones.

Ava, Malik's classmate, had always seemed to clash with him. Their personalities clashed like oil and water, and their interactions often escalated into heated arguments. Their disagreements stemmed from their differing perspectives and occasional misunderstandings about varying social issues, leaving a lingering tension between them.

Travis was adamant that the friction between the two was rooted in a secret crush. Although Malik told Travis that Ava was beautiful on the first day of school, since Malik hooked up with Mariah, there's been nothing but conflict between him and Ava.

The surprise of seeing her at his performance momentarily distracted him. Travis nudged Malik, breaking his reverie. "Ready, man?" he whispered, his voice filled with a mix of excitement and nerves.

Malik took a deep breath, letting the energy of the room fill his lungs. "Yeah, let's do this," he replied, his voice laced with determination.

Backstage, they exchanged a few final words of encouragement, their voices hushed but filled with purpose. "Remember, Malik, this is our moment," Travis said, his eyes gleaming with anticipation. "We've poured our hearts and souls into this. Let's show them who we are." "Lock in, Bro!"

Malik nodded, a newfound resolve settling within him. "You're right, Travis. It's time to let our music speak for itself. Tonight, we'll break down the barriers and share our truth with the world."

The stage manager called their names, signaling that it was their turn to shine. As they stepped onto the stage, the room erupted with applause, cheers, and whistles. The vibrant lights illuminated their path, casting a spotlight on their journey of self-discovery and resilience.

As the beat dropped and the music filled the room, Malik and Travis moved in perfect synchrony, their energy and passion radiating from every pore. The lyrics poured forth from Malik's lips with confidence, each word a testament to the battles fought, the dreams pursued, and the unyielding determination that had brought them to this moment.

"From the streets to the stage, I rise,
    In every word, a piece of paradise.
    With roots that run deep, my spirit soars,
    Reggae rhythms, hip-hop roars.

I'm a walking revolution, breaking the mold,
    Embracing my story, as it unfolds.
    I refuse to conform, I'm breaking through the chains,
    In this rap of self-expression, I'll forever remain.

So let your soul speak, let your words be heard,
    Break free from the labels, let your voice be stirred.
    You're a warrior too, let your spirit ignite,
    In this journey of self-discovery, shine your own light."

The audience became enraptured by their performance, their eyes fixed on the stage, their bodies swaying to the rhythm. The room pulsed with energy, a symphony of emotions filling the space as Malik and Travis commanded the stage. Among them, Ava stood, her previous animosity momentarily forgotten as she was drawn into the magnetic atmosphere.

With each verse, Malik's performance became a conduit for shared experiences and emotions. The power of his music transcended their past conflicts, reminding them both of the universal struggles they faced as young individuals navigating a complex world.

Backstage, Malik's mom and Mariah exchanged excited glances, their hands clasped together in anticipation. "He's incredible," Mariah whispered, her voice filled with awe. "Malik is truly finding his voice, and it's beautiful to witness."

Mom nodded, a proud smile gracing her lips. "Yes, he's shining tonight. His music is like a beacon, drawing us all closer and reminding us of the power within."

As the final notes of their performance reverberated through the air, a moment of silence hung in the room, before erupting into thunderous applause. The audience rose to their feet, their cheers and applause echoing off the walls, a testament to the impact Malik and Travis had made.

Malik looked out at the sea of faces, his heart bursting with gratitude. He gave J.R., Ma and his dad a head nod, then locked eyes with Ava. A moment of understanding passed between them, as if the weight of their past conflicts had been momentarily lifted. They had both witnessed a transformation – Malik finding his voice, and Ava witnessing the vulnerable yet empowering expression of his artistry.

Backstage, Malik and Travis shared an embrace, their hearts overflowing with a mix of relief, joy, and gratitude. "We did it," Malik whispered, his voice filled with disbelief and pride.

Travis grinned, his eyes shining with unspoken words. "We showed them, man. We showed them the power of our music and the strength of our friendship."

Mariah rushed to his side, her eyes shimmering with pride. "Bae, that was incredible! You moved me!" Malik wrapped his arms around her, holding her close. "Thank you, Bae. Your presence means everything to me. We're in this together."

"You moved everyone in that room", his mom added. "I'm so proud of you Malik."

As they stepped off the stage, their friends and family rushed forward, enveloping them in hugs and praise. Among the crowd, Ava approached Malik, a mix of admiration and humility in her eyes. "That was amazing, Malik," she said, her voice filled with sincerity. "Your music, it touched something deep within me."

Malik smiled, his heart swelling with a newfound sense of connection. "Thank you, Ava. I'm glad we could share this moment together."

And in that moment, as the music continued to reverberate through the room, Malik realized that their performance had not only touched the audience, but it had also begun to heal the rift between him and Ava. It was a reminder that music had the power to bridge divides, dissolve differences, and bring people together in ways they never thought possible.

As the event came to a close, Malik and Travis found themselves surrounded by friends and community members, all eager to share their appreciation for the music that had moved them.

Amidst the celebration, Ma approached Malik, her eyes filled with a profound sense of knowing. She embraced him, her touch a gentle reminder of the strength and wisdom that ran through their family.

"Malik, my boy, I am proud of the man you are becoming," Ma said, her voice carrying the weight of generations.

"Your music, it carries the spirit of our ancestors. May it and your connection with the creator continue to guide you on your journey. This is just a glimpse of what you can do if you put your mind to it."

Tears welled in Malik's eyes as he held onto Ma's words, his heart filled with gratitude for the unyielding support and love that surrounded him. In that moment, he understood the power of his music—to bridge the gaps between cultures, to honor his heritage, and to inspire others to embrace their own unique identities.

As Malik looked around at the joyful faces, he knew that the harmony of his struggles, the fusion of his diverse influences, had led him to this moment. With his family, his friends, and the rhythm of his music intertwining, Malik was ready to embark on a new chapter—one where his voice, steeped in cultural richness, would continue to have a positive impact on the world around him.

Malik knew that this was only the beginning of his journey. His music had become a conduit for self-expression, a vehicle for change, and a source of hope for all those who felt unseen and unheard. He and Travis would continue to create, inspire, and uplift, using their voices and their music to ignite a flame of resilience and passion in the hearts of others. For them, and their growing circle of supporters, this was just the crescendo of their journey, the beat that would propel them forward, united in rhythm and resolve.

Chapter 6: Musical Interlude

alik's heart sank as' the words echoed through the classroom. Although he was gaining momentum with his music and looked forward to his time mixing beats with Travis, schooled remained a low point in his day and his lackluster attitude was about to cost him.

Detention!

It was a consequence he had hoped to avoid, but his behavior had crossed the line, and now he had to face the consequences. As the final bell rang, he reluctantly gathered his belongings and made his way to the designated detention room.

As Malik sat in the after-school detention room, he couldn't help but feel trapped within its walls. The room was small and dimly lit, with fluorescent lights flickering overhead. The windows were covered with heavy blinds, blocking out any glimpse of the outside world. The air felt stale and suffocating, carrying a faint scent of disinfectant.

The room was sparsely furnished, with a few mismatched tables and chairs arranged haphazardly. The chairs were uncomfortable, their worn-out cushions offering little support. The walls were bare, except for a faded motivational poster that had seen better days.

The silence in the room was deafening, broken only by the distant sound of students' voices echoing through the hallway. The absence of any distractions or forms of entertainment only amplified the feeling of confinement. It was as if time stood still within those four walls, emphasizing the weight of Malik's actions and the consequences he faced.

Malik couldn't help but feel a mix of frustration and disappointment in himself. He had let his emotions get the best of him, reacting impulsively to a situation that could have been handled differently. As he sat in silence, he reflected on his actions, realizing the impact they had not only on himself but also on those around him.

Detention became a regular routine. The hours spent confined to the room allowed him time for introspection and self-reflection. He began to question his choices, recognizing the importance of controlling his emotions and finding healthier ways to express himself.

While Malik's detention served as a punishment, it also became an unexpected opportunity for growth. With each passing day, he developed a fresh sense of discipline and maturity. He used the time to delve into his passion for music, writing lyrics and honing his rap skills. The words flowed from his pen, becoming a cathartic release, a channel for his frustrations and a pathway to self-discovery.

But just as Malik started to find purpose and joy in his new outlet, his world took another blow. He returned home to find his parents waiting for him, disappointment clearly visible on their faces.

"Hand over the phone Son", Dad growled. "You are Grounded." Malik knew then that Ms. Jackson had informed them that he was caught with his phone out while in Detention which was prohibited. The punishment seemed fitting, as his parents explained the impact of his actions and the importance of acting with integrity and being responsible.

With his cell phone confiscated and his social activities limited, Malik was forced to confront his own choices and confront his own demons. The absence of his phone left a void, but it also allowed him to reevaluate his priorities.

The next day, Malik sat in detention after school, the monotony of the room brought forth memories of a time long ago. His mind traveled back to his middle school years, a period marked by significant changes and challenges that shaped his journey.

Once upon a time, Malik had been an outgoing and energetic child. He had a natural talent for drumming and would spend hours lost in the rhythms and beats. Music was his refuge, a way to express himself and connect with others. He was content, surrounded by friends who shared his passion for music and a sense of camaraderie.

But everything changed when Malik had to switch schools. His family had relocated to a different neighborhood, one that was unfamiliar and socially and economically different from his previous surroundings. Suddenly, Malik found himself in a sea of new faces, unfamiliar customs, and different interests. The once vibrant and confident boy became a hesitant and withdrawn teenager.

The stark contrast in social status between Malik and his new peers ignited a battle within him. He struggled with feelings of inadequacy, believing he didn't fit in or belong. His self-worth became entangled in material possessions, as he saw his classmates flaunt designer clothes, expensive gadgets, and lavish lifestyles. Malik felt left out and insecure, unable to keep up with the ever-changing trends and consumerist culture.

The weight of these comparisons and the pressure to conform to societal standards began to take a toll on Malik's mental health. He battled with depression, feeling isolated and lost in a world that seemed to value superficiality over authenticity. The once vibrant beats of his drums now echoed with a sense of emptiness.

Recognizing the depth of his struggle, Malik's parents sought the help of a counselor. They believed in the power of seeking guidance and understanding to navigate the complexities of adolescence. Malik hesitantly attended counseling sessions, unsure of what to expect or whether it would make any difference.

The counselor, a wise and empathetic figure, understood the pain and confusion that Malik carried within him. Through their conversations, Malik began to peel back the layers of self-doubt and societal pressure that had engulfed him. The counselor gently guided him to embrace his uniqueness, encouraging him to be true to himself and find his own path.

In those counseling sessions, Malik discovered the profound truth that his worth as an individual couldn't be measured by material possessions or societal standards. He learned to appreciate his own talents, interests, and perspectives, understanding that his uniqueness was a strength, not a weakness. The counselor's words became a mantra for Malik: "You are enough. Embrace your individuality and let it shine."

As Malik continued his journey, he gradually let go of the need for validation from others. He reconnected with his love for drumming, not as a means to fit in, but as a genuine expression of his passion. Through music, he found solace and an avenue for self-expression that transcended the boundaries of social expectations.

Over time, Malik's sense of self-worth and acceptance began to radiate from within. He no longer sought approval from his peers or compared himself to others. Instead, he focused on nurturing genuine connections based on shared values and interests.

The experiences of his father served as a source of inspiration and encouragement for Malik. He learned that his dad had faced similar struggles during his own middle school years, but had emerged stronger and more resilient. The knowledge that his father had overcome those challenges gave Malik the confidence to navigate his own path.

As the flashback dissolved, Malik found himself back in the detention room, but with a fresh perspective. The journey he had traveled, filled with self-discovery, challenges, and growth, had shaped him into the person he was today. He understood that his sense of self-worth couldn't be defined by external factors, but rather by embracing his uniqueness and staying true to himself.

With a renewed sense of purpose, Malik was determined to continue his journey of self-discovery and resilience. He carried the wisdom gained from the counseling sessions with him, cherishing the value of his individuality and the power of self-acceptance. Malik was ready to face the world, no longer burdened by the weight of comparison, but instead celebrating his own journey and embracing the path that lay ahead.

The weeks went by, and Malik's stint in detention and grounding gradually came to an end. As Dad returned his cell phone and lifted his restrictions, he felt an appreciation for the opportunities it provided, but also a newfound understanding of the need to use the things he had and his freedom responsibly and mindfully.

The experience of detention and grounding left an indelible mark on Malik's journey. He learned that mistakes were not the end, but rather stepping stones towards growth and self-improvement. He emerged from the process with a deeper understanding of his emotions, a heightened sense of responsibility, and a determination to make better choices.

Detention and grounding had initially felt like punishment, but in hindsight, they became catalysts for positive change. Malik learned to channel his emotions into his music, embracing the power of his voice and the impact it could have on others. The experience deepened his resolve to use his talents to inspire, uplift, and bring about positive change in his community.

Chapter 7: Melodies of Resilience

The city's skyline painted a breathtaking backdrop as Malik and Travis walked through the bustling streets of Harmonyville. Their music had gained momentum, spreading through the local community like wildfire. The once-struggling teenager had discovered his voice, and now, he and Travis were on a mission to inspire others with their melodies of resilience.

Their latest track, "Rise Above," had struck a chord with listeners—a powerful anthem that spoke of overcoming obstacles and defying the odds. The song's message hit deeply, reflecting the struggles faced not only by Malik but also by individuals from all walks of life.

As they navigated the city, a familiar face appeared in their path. It was J.R., Malik's younger brother, his face illuminated by the glow of his handheld gaming device. J.R. had always admired Malik's musical journey, quietly observing his older brother's transformation from a distance.

"Hey, J.R.!" Malik called out, a smile spreading across his face.

"How's the game going?"

J.R. looked up, a grin stretching across his face. "Bro, I finally beat the final boss! This game was intense."

Malik chuckled, patting J.R. on the back. "That's awesome, little man. Congrats! Hey, have you heard our latest track?"

J.R.'s eyes lit up with curiosity. "No way! You guys made another song?"

Travis nodded, excitement shining in his eyes. "Absolutely, J.R.! Let's give it a listen."

As they stood on the sidewalk, Malik pulled his portable speaker from his bag and synced it with his cell phone and let "Rise Above" ring out. The empowering lyrics and infectious beats filled the air, capturing J.R.'s attention. His eyes widened, and his head started to nod along with the rhythm. The song's message struck to the core, echoing the challenges he faced in his own life.

"Wow, bro, that's amazing!" J.R. exclaimed, his voice filled with admiration. "You guys are really making a difference with your music. I'm proud of you."

Malik's heart swelled with joy. To know that his music touched not only his peers but also his younger brother, inspiring him to persevere, was a testament to the power of their melodies of resilience.

Months went by and the demand for Malik and Travis's music grew. They were invited to perform at local community events, school assemblies, and even youth empowerment conferences. The city had embraced their music as a beacon of hope and empowerment.

One afternoon, as Malik was checking his messages, he received a heartfelt note from a young girl named Olivia. Her words struck him to the core as she shared her struggles with self-doubt, depression, and thoughts of self-harm. The weight of her words settled heavily upon him, igniting a sense of urgency to reach out and offer support.

Malik took a deep breath, determined to make a difference. He replied to Olivia's message, expressing his gratitude for her honesty and courage in opening up. He urged her to seek help from trusted adults, counselors, or helplines available to provide support in challenging times. He assured her that she was not alone and that there were people who cared and wanted to help her through her struggles.

Inspired by Olivia's message and the knowledge that their music could offer hope to those in need, Malik decided to organize a community event—a "Melodies of Resilience" concert that would not only celebrate the power of music but also raise awareness about mental health support resources. The goal was to create a safe space where people could come together, share their stories, and find comfort in the melodies that had touched their hearts.

As the day of the concert arrived, the venue buzzed with anticipation. Friends, family, and members of the community filled the space, eagerly awaiting the performances that would tell the story of their own journeys of resilience.

Malik and Travis took the stage, the spotlight illuminating their faces. They shared the stories behind their songs, spoke of their personal struggles, and encouraged everyone in the audience to embrace their own unique voices. And then, they performed—their music filling the room, hearts swelling with every beat.

One by one, individuals from the community took the stage, sharing their own stories of triumph and perseverance. A young artist unveiled a painting that captured her journey through mental health challenges. A poet recited verses that echoed the pain and healing of her past. The atmosphere was charged with emotion, a collective spirit of resilience weaving through the room.

As the concert drew to a close, Malik addressed the crowd, his voice filled with gratitude and determination. "Thank you all for being here tonight. Together, we've created a space where our stories intertwine, where the melodies of resilience echo through our hearts. Let us continue to rise above, to uplift one another, and to embrace the power of our voices."

The room erupted in applause, a symphony of appreciation and unity. Malik glanced at Travis, their eyes meeting—a shared understanding of the impact they had made, and the responsibility they carried to continue spreading the melodies of resilience.

As they walked through the streets of their city, the melodies of resilience continued to echo in their hearts. Together, Malik and Travis knew that they had found their purpose—to uplift, to inspire, and to remind others that within every struggle, there existed a melody waiting to be heard. And they were determined to be there for those who needed support, just like Olivia, spreading hope through their music and extending a helping hand to those who were struggling, ensuring that no one felt alone in their battles.

The next day at school, as Malik sat in the back of the classroom, lost in his own thoughts, Ms. Bing approached him with a twinkle in her eye. "Malik," she said, "I have a special project for you." Hearing about the "Melodies of Resilience" concert and aware of the transformation taking place in Malik's attitude outside of school, she thought she could leverage that momentum to help him with his academic experience.

Malik raised an eyebrow, skeptical of what could be so special about another assignment. "What is it, Ms. Bing?" he asked with a hint of caution.

With a smile, Ms. Bing explained that she wanted Malik to write an original poem and share it with the class. She believed in his talent for storytelling through words, and she wanted him to embrace his creative side fully.

Malik's initial reaction was resistance. The thought of standing in front of his classmates, baring his soul through poetry, filled him with a mix of fear and vulnerability. But deep down, he knew this was an opportunity to break free from his self-imposed limitations.

Reluctantly, Malik accepted the challenge. He poured his heart and soul into crafting a poem that reflected his journey of self-discovery, resilience, and the power of creative expression. It became a lyrical testament to his struggles and triumphs, a piece that captured the essence of his unique voice.

The day of the presentation arrived, and Malik stood before his classmates, his palms sweaty and his heart pounding. As he began reciting his poem, he felt a surge of adrenaline coursing through his veins. The words flowed effortlessly, each line resonating with his own experiences and emotions.

As he finished his recitation, there was a moment of silence, followed by applause that erupted from his classmates. They were moved by the honesty and raw emotion in Malik's words.

Ms. Bing beamed with pride, her belief in Malik's talent fully validated. She saw the transformation happening before her eyes—the hesitant, troubled student was blossoming into a confident young artist.

Ms. Bing shared the poem with other teachers who shared it with their students. The Librarian went as far as to frame a copy and hang it up in the entrance to the school library. His poems became a source of inspiration for those who felt silenced, giving them the courage to embrace their own journeys of self-discovery and self-expression.

In the end, Malik realized that the special project assigned by Ms.

Bing was not just an assignment—it was a pivotal moment in his life. It ignited a passion within him, a fire that would continue to burn brightly as he embarked on his artistic path.

From that day forward, Malik's perception of himself shifted at school. He no longer saw himself as just a troubled student, but as a poet, a storyteller, and a voice that could inspire others. Writing became his outlet, a way to express his thoughts, dreams, and fears with honesty and vulnerability and help. Although he still had to work twice as hard academically and would still get frustrated from time to time, his writing had a way of helping him overcome feelings of being a failure at everything.

In months that followed, Malik and Travis continued their musical journey, inspired by the connections they had forged and the lives they had touched. Their melodies traveled far beyond the boundaries of Harmonyville, reaching individuals from all walks of life who found solace, hope, and strength within their music.

Chapter 8: Crafting the Anthem

The air crackled with anticipation as Malik and Travis huddled together in their basement studio. The time had come to create something truly extraordinary—an anthem that would encapsulate the spirit of resilience and inspire all who heard it. The room buzzed with creative energy, their shared passion fueling their determination.

Malik flipped open his notebook, his lyrics inscribed across the pages like a road map of his journey. He began to recite his verses, his voice infused with the fire of his experiences.

"In the depths of my soul, I find a story untold,
A tale of self-worth, identity, and self-expression bold.
For I am a warrior, a poet in the making,
With words as my armor, and truth my undertaking.

In a world that seeks to label and define,
I refuse to be confined, my spirit won't resign.
For I am a symphony, a kaleidoscope of hues,
An amalgamation of dreams, an array of infinite views.

I am not defined by the judgments they cast,
   I stand tall, unshaken, for I'm built to last.
   I am the whisper of courage, the echo of a voice,
   I reclaim my power, make my own choice.

No longer will I shrink to fit their narrow design,
   I'll rise like a phoenix, let my spirit intertwine.
   For self-worth lies within, a treasure to unveil,
   Embracing my flaws, I'll set sail, I won't fail."

Travis's eyes sparkled with excitement, his fingers itching to create the perfect beat that would elevate Malik's words to new heights. "Man, those lyrics are gold, Malik. Let's bring them to life. This anthem will speak to the entire community."

They spent hours fine-tuning the melody, experimenting with different arrangements and instruments. Each note became a brushstroke on the canvas of their shared vision—a tapestry of sound that would inspire hope and ignite change.

As they crafted the anthem, news of Malik's journey began to spread throughout the community. His peers, friends, and even family members were captivated by his story and the power of his music. People were drawn to the authenticity and passion that emanated from his words, finding comfort and inspiration in his melodies.

One evening, as Malik and Travis took a break from their creative process, a knock resounded through the studio door. Malik opened it to find a familiar face standing there—Marcus "LyricalFlow" Johnson, Malik's favorite rapper, from their very own neighborhood.

"Yo, Malik!" Marcus exclaimed, his charismatic presence filling the room. "I've been hearing about your journey, man. Your music is making waves in the community, I was back home visiting the fam and I had to come and check it out for myself."

Malik's eyes widened with disbelief and excitement. Marcus was a legend in their neighborhood, renowned for his lyrical prowess and storytelling abilities. To have him standing in their studio was an honor beyond words.

"Marcus, it's an honor to have you here," Malik stammered, his voice filled with admiration. "You've been such an inspiration to me. Your music speaks to my soul."

Marcus grinned, his confidence radiating. "I appreciate the love, Malik. But let me tell you something—you got talent. Real talent. Your words have power, and I believe in you. I see potential."

Malik's heart swelled with gratitude. To be acknowledged by his idol, someone who had achieved success while staying true to their roots, was a validation of his journey. Marcus's presence ignited a fire within him, fueling his determination to make an impact with his music.

Marcus's admiration for Malik's talent and his dedication to uplifting aspiring artists like him were evident. He had walked a similar path, coming from a middle-class background and breaking through the barriers to success. Marcus recognized the importance of giving back to the community that had shaped him, and he saw Malik as a promising artist who could carry the torch forward.

"Malik, I want to help you craft this anthem," Marcus declared, his voice filled with conviction. "Together, we can make something powerful, something that will shake the foundations and inspire a generation."

Malik's eyes shone with excitement as he nodded, his voice filled with determination. "I would be honored, Marcus. Let's create something that will shake the community, something that will ignite change." And so, Malik and Marcus joined forces, their creative energies intertwining as they shaped the anthem.

As the evening unfolded, Malik and Travis found themselves engrossed in conversation with Marcus. He shared stories of his own musical journey, recounting the challenges he had faced and the triumphs he had celebrated along the way. They listened with rapt attention, hanging onto every word, as Marcus painted vivid pictures of his early days as an aspiring artist.

He spoke of humble beginnings, performing at small local venues and open mic nights, where he honed his craft and built a loyal fan base. Marcus reminisced about the late nights spent writing lyrics in his cramped apartment, the melodies that flowed through him like a divine gift. He described the moments of self-doubt and frustration, when the world seemed indifferent to his talent, but he never lost faith in his ability to make a difference through his music.

The challenges Marcus faced were not just external, but also internal. He opened up about the doubts and insecurities that plagued him, the moments of questioning his own worth and relevance in the ever-evolving music industry. Yet, through it all, he persevered, using his experiences as fuel to push himself further, to grow as an artist, and to create music that resonated with others.

As the night wore on, the conversation shifted to the crafting of the Anthem—the defining piece that would capture the essence of their journey and unite their community. Marcus's presence brought a fresh perspective to the process, his wisdom and experience guiding their creative exploration.

However, the road to creating the Anthem was not without its challenges. As Malik, Travis, and Marcus dove deeper into their artistic collaboration, they encountered moments of creative differences and clashes of vision. Each of them brought their own unique style and approach to the table, leading to occasional tensions and disagreements.

At times, doubts began to creep into Malik's mind. He questioned whether he had the skill and expertise to contribute meaningfully to such a monumental project. The weight of expectation and the fear of not living up to the standards set by Marcus and their community burdened him. It was a test of his confidence and ability to trust his own artistic instincts.

But instead of letting these challenges consume them, Malik, Travis, and Marcus embraced them as opportunities for growth and collaboration. They engaged in passionate debates, challenged each other's perspectives, and allowed their individual strengths to shine through. Through this process, they discovered an untapped synergy, a creative energy that flowed seamlessly between them.

Late nights turned into early mornings as they meticulously crafted the Anthem, pouring their hearts and souls into each line, each note. Their shared experiences, struggles, and triumphs served as the foundation, infusing the lyrics with an authenticity and emotional depth that resonated with their audience.

The studio became a sanctuary of creativity and collaboration. Instruments were played with fervor, lyrics were revised and refined, and melodies were carefully crafted to evoke the desired emotions. The walls reverberated with their collective passion, as if the very essence of their music had taken physical form within the space.

Outside the studio, the anticipation for the Anthem grew. The community eagerly awaited the release, their hopes pinned on the promise of a unifying anthem that would amplify their voices and shed light on their shared experiences. Malik, Travis, and Marcus felt the weight of responsibility on their shoulders, but also the exhilaration of the impact their music could have.

The day of the Anthem's release arrived, accompanied by a mix of nerves and excitement. The community center buzzed with anticipation as they prepared for the unveiling. Malik stood on stage, flanked by Travis and Marcus, their bond fortified by their shared journey. The air crackled with electricity, an energy that could only be described as the culmination of countless hours of dedication, collaboration, and resilience.

As the first notes of the Anthem filled the room, a wave of emotion washed over Malik. He felt the power of his words, the melodies taking on a life of their own. The crowd erupted in applause, their hearts resonating with the message of hope. They started to They sing along, their voices merging into a chorus of unity and strength. Tears streamed down Malik's face, his heart overflowing with a sense of purpose and fulfillment.

The Anthem became an instant sensation, resonating deeply with the community and beyond. Its words, melodies, and uplifting message became a source of inspiration for those who had felt unheard and overlooked. It ignited conversations, sparked movements, and became a rallying cry for change. Malik realized that his journey had transcended his personal aspirations. He had become a symbol of inspiration, a beacon of hope for those who needed it. With the guidance and support of Marcus, he had embraced his own passions and, in turn, encouraged others to do the same.

For Malik, Travis, and Marcus, the journey didn't end with the success of the Anthem. It was just the beginning—a launching pad for their future endeavors and a reminder of the power of their collective voices. They continued to create music that touched hearts, inspired minds, and united communities, forever connected by the symphony they had orchestrated together.

As they looked back on their shared journey, Malik, Travis, and Marcus knew that the challenges they had faced along the way had only served to strengthen their resolve. They had overcome doubts, navigated creative differences, and stayed true to their artistic visions. Through their music, they had discovered not only their own voices, but also the power of music to bring people together, to spark change, and to create a symphony of resilience, hope, and belonging.

Chapter 9: Symphony of Revelation

The sun-drenched rays pierced through the windows as Malik's family piled into the car, excitement brewing in the air. It was time for a much-needed getaway, an escape from the pressures and expectations of everyday life. The destination? A secluded campsite nestled deep within the heart of the sprawling countryside.

As they embarked on their journey, the landscape gradually transformed from the concrete jungle to a vibrant tapestry of rolling hills and lush greenery. The road meandered through picturesque valleys, flanked by towering trees that whispered secrets to the wind. The scent of wildflowers permeated the air, igniting a sense of freedom and adventure.

After a few hours of driving, they arrived at the campsite—a hidden oasis tucked away from the hustle and bustle of the city. The serenity of the location washed over them as they stepped out of the car, their eyes widening in awe at the breathtaking beauty surrounding them.

The campsite boasted an idyllic lake, its crystal-clear waters shimmering under the golden rays of the setting sun. Around the perimeter of the lake, towering cliffs rose majestically, their rugged faces a testament to the passage of time. In the distance, dense forests beckoned, inviting exploration and discovery.

Malik's dad, a seasoned outdoors-man, wasted no time in unpacking their arsenal of adventure gear. Dirt bikes, ATV's, and 4-wheelers stood in a row, ready to be unleashed upon the untamed terrain that awaited them. The metallic roar of engines mingled with the symphony of nature, creating a harmonious melody that echoed through the wilderness.

With helmets fastened and adrenaline coursing through their veins, Malik and his family embarked on their wild escapade. The wind whipped against their faces as they carved through winding trails, their laughter mingling with the sounds of roaring engines and crunching leaves beneath their tires.

The freedom of the open landscape provided a respite from the constraints of their everyday lives. For Malik, it was an opportunity to let go of his worries, to lose himself in the exhilarating rush of adrenaline. With each twist and turn, his spirits soared, and the weight that had burdened him began to lift.

As the sun dipped below the horizon, casting hues of orange and pink across the sky, they returned to their campsite, their bodies tingling with exhaustion and euphoria. The crackling fire offered warmth and comfort, its dancing flames casting playful shadows across their faces.

Underneath the star-studded canopy of the night sky, they sat around the campfire, basking in its warm glow. The crackling embers created a symphony of soothing sounds, inviting them to let their guards down and embrace vulnerability. The ambiance of the night seemed to coax secrets from the depths of their souls.

In this moment of serenity, Malik found himself opening up to his family like never before. He spoke of the battles he had fought within himself, the doubts and insecurities that had plagued his mind. He shared his struggles with his mental health, the moments when he felt lost and disconnected from his own identity.

His voice trembled with raw emotion as he described the profound impact music had on his journey of self-discovery. With tears glistening in his eyes, he spoke of the solace he found in crafting lyrics that carried the weight of his experiences, transforming pain into powerful messages of resilience and hope.

As Malik poured out his heart, his family listened with unwavering support and understanding. His dad, a pillar of strength, wrapped him in a tight embrace, his voice gruff with emotion. "Son," he said, his voice filled with paternal love, "you've been carrying so much on your shoulders, but remember that you don't have to face it alone. We're here for you, every step of the way."

His mom, her eyes shimmering with tears, added, "Malik, you are a shining star in this world. Your journey, though difficult, has molded you into a remarkable young man. Your struggles do not define you; they have shaped you into someone with a deep well of empathy and strength."

Even J.R., his younger brother, chimed in, his voice filled with youthful wisdom. "Malik, you inspire me every day. Your music touches my soul, and I know it touches others too. Keep pouring your heart into those lyrics, and never stop being true to yourself."

In that vulnerable moment, surrounded by the embrace of his family, Malik felt a sense of acceptance and love that he had yearned for. The weight that had burdened his heart began to dissipate, replaced by a sense of purpose and belonging.

As the campfire crackled and the night grew darker, they continued to share stories, laughter, and the melodies of their hearts. The flickering flames danced in rhythm with their voices, painting an intimate portrait of a family united in love and support.

In the midst of the wilderness, Malik found himself not only embracing the untamed beauty of nature but also rediscovering the untamed spirit within himself. The weekend getaway had become a transformative journey, a sanctuary of self-discovery and healing.

In the days that followed, as they packed up their belongings and bid farewell to the campsite, Malik felt a renewed sense of purpose. He knew that he would continue to face challenges, but he now carried with him the unwavering support of his family and the realization that his music had the power to touch lives.

As they drove away, the landscape slowly fading into the distance, Malik looked out the window with a smile on his face. The memories of their weekend getaway were etched into his heart, serving as a reminder of the strength that resided within him and the unbreakable bond of love that surrounded him.

With each passing mile, he felt a surge of gratitude and determination. The road ahead may be filled with twists and turns, but armed with his family's unwavering love and the power of his music, Malik knew that he would navigate it with resilience, purpose, and a wild spirit that would never be tamed. He was rejuvenated and anxious to get back to the city. An earlier message from Travis had him a little worried.

Chapter 10: Crescendo of Confidence

The crisp autumn air carried a sense of excitement as Malik entered Travis's room. It had been a challenging week for both of them, especially for Travis, who now sported a cast on his foot after a car accident he got into while Malik was gone on vacation.

Travis had always been an adventurous spirit, and the day of the accident was no exception. Behind the wheel of his dad's sleek Mustang, he felt an exhilarating sense of freedom as he cruised down the open road. Little did he know that a split-second distraction would change everything.

Engrossed in a phone call, Travis's attention wavered from the road ahead. In that momentary lapse, he swerved into the adjacent lane, colliding with another car. The impact was jarring, the screeching sound of metal against metal piercing the air.

Time seemed to freeze as Travis realized the gravity of his mistake. Panic surged through his veins as he saw the frightened face of the young teen in the other car. She was shaken but thankfully unharmed. Relief washed over him, mingling with guilt and remorse for the negligence that had caused the accident.

Emergency services had arrived swiftly, ensuring both drivers were safe. Travis was taken to the hospital for observation, his body checked for hidden injuries. It turned out that he had been fortunate, escaping major harm. The only visible evidence of the accident was a cast now encasing his foot.

During his time in the hospital, Travis reflected on the accident with a heavy heart. He couldn't shake the guilt that weighed upon him. Determined to make amends, he wrote a heartfelt letter to the young teen, expressing his deepest apologies and sincere remorse. He wanted her to know that he understood the impact his actions had on her, and he vowed to be more responsible in the future.

Malik was grateful that the situation was not worse and that Travis had learned from his mistake. Despite the setback, they were determined to keep the momentum of their music going. As Malik settled into a chair beside Travis's bed, he couldn't help but admire his friend's resolve.

"Man, I can't believe you're still pushing forward, even with that cast," Malik said, a mix of awe and concern in his voice.

Travis grinned, his eyes sparkling with determination.
    "Life is about learning and growing, Malik. Each day another opportunity to do things better. To be better", he said as he turned his gaze towards a family photo next to a small mixer on his desk.

"Nothing can hold us back, bro. Not even a foot cast. We've come too far to let this slow us down."

Malik nodded, a surge of admiration filling his heart. Travis's unwavering spirit had always been a source of inspiration, and now, faced with adversity, his friend's resolve only grew stronger.

Their friendship had blossomed through their shared passion for music, and it had become an anchor for both of them on their respective journeys. Through the ups and downs, they had supported and encouraged one another, celebrating victories and offering refuge during moments of doubt.

Malik's family had also played a crucial role in his pursuit of music. His mom, dad, and J.R. had become his biggest cheerleaders, unwavering in their support. They attended every performance, whether it was at a local community event or a small gathering in their basement studio.

One evening, as Malik worked on new lyrics in his room, his mom knocked gently on the door. She entered with a warm smile, a warm tray of cookies Dad had just pulled out the oven in hand. Malik set aside his notebook and greeted her.

"Hey, Mom. What's up?" he asked, his voice filled with curiosity.

His mom placed the tray on his desk and took a seat beside him. "I've been watching you, Malik. Your dedication and passion for music are truly remarkable. I want you to know that your father and I are incredibly proud of you."

A mixture of gratitude and relief washed over Malik. His parents' unwavering support had bolstered his confidence, providing him with the strength to pursue his dreams. Their words of encouragement sank deep within his heart, reaffirming his purpose.

"Thanks, Mom," Malik said, his voice filled with emotion. "I couldn't have come this far without your support. It means the world to me."

His mom placed a hand on his shoulder, her eyes shining with pride. "Remember, Malik, music has the power to bring people together, to heal wounds, and to inspire change. Keep using your voice to make a difference."

Malik nodded, feeling a renewed sense of purpose. His mom's words reminding him of the impact he could make with his music. He was determined to continue using his voice to uplift others and bridge gaps within his community.

The accident had brought about a temporary change in the dynamics between Malik and Travis. With Travis unable to attend practice sessions or join Malik in performances, they found new ways to strengthen their bond. They spent hours on video chat, discussing lyrics, brainstorming ideas, and supporting each other's creative endeavors.

One afternoon, as Malik arrived at Travis's house, he was greeted by the sight of Travis sitting on his front porch with his foot elevated. Malik couldn't help but notice the glum expression on his friend's face.

"What's up, man? You seem a bit down," Malik said, taking a seat beside him.

Travis let out a sigh. "I miss being able to contribute fully, you know? It's frustrating not being able to perform with you. I feel like I'm letting you down."

Malik placed a reassuring hand on Travis's shoulder. "Hey, don't even think like that. We're a team, and setbacks happen. Your presence alone inspires me, and your support means everything. We'll get through this together."

Travis's face brightened, gratitude shining in his eyes. "Thanks, bro. I needed to hear that. You're right—we're in this together. I guess some days I am more positive than others. I was just giving you a pep talk, now here I am all up in my feelings." They both laughed.

"Let's keep making music, no matter the circumstances."

With renewed determination, Malik and Travis continued their musical journey. Malik dedicated himself to writing lyrics that reflected their bond, emphasizing their friendship and the strength they found in each other. They channeled their experiences, including the challenges they faced, into their music, creating a tapestry of resilience and unity.

Months passed and Malik lit up the stage at a few local parties without his trusted collaborator and personal DJ, but always gave Travis a shout-out who he knew would be watching from one of the hundreds of live streams on social media. While Malik was finding purpose in his music, he still struggled and was not as motivated as he should be academically. He needed to maintain passing grades, or his Dad would not allow him to perform.

Desperate, he heeded his parents recommendation of after school tutoring. However, he was not going to sit in the free tutoring sessions offered after school. He refused to spend any extra time at Winston High. He asked Mariah to be his tutor and help him stay on track. The two decided that Saturday mornings worked best since Mariah was busy with design class most evenings.

One Saturday as Malik sat on his bed across from Mariah, staring and smiling at her as she broke down a complicated math formula, he spoke out, "How did I get so lucky?" Pausing in mid-sentence, Mariah looked up, her cheeks already turning red.

"Through all of my struggles at school and finding my identity, you have been my safe place, my confidant, and my biggest supporter. Your unwavering belief in me, even when I doubted myself, has been a constant source of strength. You've cheered me on during my lowest moments and celebrated my every success."

"Your intelligence, beauty, and kind heart inspire me every day, he continued.

"I can't imagine my life without you by my side. Together, we've navigated the twists and turns of this journey, and I am grateful for every moment we've shared. You are my rock, my muse, and the melody to my lyrics. I know things have been a little crazy lately, but I need you to know I love you more than words can express, and I'm excited to continue writing our story together."

Mariah's eyes welled up with tears of joy as she leaned in to embrace Malik, their hearts beating in sync, knowing that their love and support would continue to strengthen them as they embraced the future, united in their dreams and aspirations. Studying with Mariah had help Malik pull most of his grades up which meant he kept Dad off his case and could continue to perform his raps.

As the day of his next performance approached, the excitement in the air was palpable. There was a charity music event being sponsored by a famous musician and Malik was invited to be the opening act.

The community had rallied around Malik, eager to witness his growth and support his unwavering passion for music. The anticipation built as the day of the charity music event drew closer. Malik's name buzzed through conversations, spreading like wildfire among friends, family, and even strangers who had heard whispers of his talent.

The venue itself was a sight to behold. It was a grand outdoor amphitheater nestled in the heart of the community, surrounded by towering trees and bathed in the warm glow of twinkling lights. The stage stood tall, waiting to be graced by the performers who would fill the air with their melodies and lyrics.

On the day of the event, Malik arrived early, his heart pounding with a mix of excitement and nervousness. He was greeted by the hum of activity as fellow musicians tuned their instruments and sound technicians made final adjustments. The backstage atmosphere was electric, with performers exchanging words of encouragement and sharing stories of their own musical journeys.

As Malik stepped onto the stage, a surge of adrenaline coursed through his veins. The crowd, a sea of eager faces, cheered in anticipation. The spotlight illuminated him, casting a warm glow that seemed to wrap around him like a comforting embrace.

He took a deep breath and let the music take over. He felt the rhythm pulsate through his veins, drawing strength from the lyrics he had crafted with Travis. And there, in the front row, sat Travis, his face beaming with pride and admiration.

With each lyric and every beat, he poured his heart and soul into his performance. The crowd was captivated, their cheers growing louder with each song. Malik's words resonated with them, weaving a tapestry of emotions that brought people together in a shared experience.

As he finished his final song, a thunderous applause erupted, shaking the very foundation of the amphitheater. The love and support from the audience washed over Malik like a tidal wave, overwhelming him with a profound sense of accomplishment and validation. Tears of joy filled his eyes as he soaked in the moment, basking in the realization that his music had touched the hearts of those around him.

But it wasn't just the audience that was moved by Malik's performance. Backstage, his family and friends gathered, their faces beaming with pride and admiration. They had witnessed his growth, his resilience, and the unwavering dedication he had poured into his craft. In that moment, they knew that Malik had found his voice, his purpose, and his place in the world.

As the event came to a close, the charity organizers took to the stage to express their gratitude to all the performers, including Malik. They praised the power of music to bring people together and create positive change in the community. The funds raised that night would go towards supporting local initiatives, offering opportunities for aspiring young artists and providing resources for mental health awareness.

Malik stepped off the stage, his heart still racing with the energy of the night. He was met with hugs, congratulations, and words of admiration from those who had witnessed his transformation. In that moment, surrounded by loved ones, he felt an overwhelming sense of gratitude for the support and love that had carried him through his journey.

As Malik and Travis basked in the afterglow of the performance and the music they had created, they knew that their journey was far from over. They had experienced the power of music to bridge gaps and heal wounds, and they were determined to continue using their voices to make a difference.

Together, they would navigate the twists and turns of their musical path, supporting and uplifting each other every step of the way. Their bond had grown unshakable, and they were ready to face any challenges that lay ahead.

Little did they know that their music and their story would continue to inspire and move others, and was reaching far beyond their immediate circle. Their bond and unwavering spirits would become an anthem for many, a reminder that bonds forged through passion and support could withstand any obstacle.

Making their way home, the stars twinkled overhead, mirroring the brightness in their hearts. The journey was still unfolding, and they were ready to embrace the chapters yet to come, united in their love for music and strengthened by the bonds they had formed along the way.

At home in his room, Malik couldn't help but reflect on how far he had come. From a troubled student plagued by self-doubt to a confident and talented artist, he had embraced his true self and found his voice. His journey had not been easy, but the challenges had shaped him into the person he was today – a person who had discovered the power of music, the resilience of the human spirit, and the unbreakable bonds of community.

Closing his eyes that night, he knew that this was just the beginning. His passion for music burned brighter than ever, and he was ready to continue sharing his voice with the world. With each new song, each new performance, and each new chapter of his life, he would carry the lessons learned and the love and support of his community in his heart. Malik had found his voice, and he was ready to let it soar.

Chapter 11: Embracing Identity and Purpose

The sun peeked through the blinds, casting a warm glow across Malik's room. As he sat at his desk, surrounded by his notebooks and the rhythm of his thoughts, he couldn't help but feel a sense of clarity and purpose. The journey he had embarked upon had led him to a deeper understanding of his own identity, and his passion for music had become a guiding force in his life.

Just as Malik was lost in thought, there was a gentle knock on his door. He turned to see his dad, dressed in his Marine Corps uniform, standing in the doorway. His dad's presence always commanded respect and admiration, and Malik's heart swelled with a mix of anticipation and nervousness.

"Hey, Dad," Malik greeted, his voice laced with curiosity.

His dad entered the room, his expression a blend of pride and concern. He took a seat beside Malik, leaning back and crossing his arms. "Son, I wanted to talk to you about something important. I've been watching your journey with music, and I have to say, I'm impressed by your dedication and talent. But I want to make sure you're staying true to yourself and your values."

Malik's brow furrowed slightly, unsure of what his dad meant. "What do you mean, Dad?"

His dad leaned forward, his eyes locked with Malik's. I overheard you comparing yourself to other artists. Son, remember comparison is cage that traps you in either feelings of inadequacy or arrogance. Either way, it stunts your growth."

If Dad had said it once, he had said it a thousands times. Malik took a deep breath has he lowered his head.
   "Look at me", he said. "Be yourself; uniquely and unapologetically. Your identity is more than just your music. It's about who you are as a person, the values you hold, and the impact you want to make in this world. Music is a powerful tool, but don't let it define you entirely."

Malik nodded, taking in his dad's words. He understood the importance of staying grounded and true to his roots, even as he pursued his passion for music. It was a reminder he needed—a reminder to remain authentic and use his voice for positive change.

His dad continued, his tone softening. "I've seen the positive impact you're already making in our community, Malik. Your music is inspiring others, and it's a testament to your dedication and perseverance. Remember that you have the power to shape not only your own identity but also the narrative of our community. Use that power wisely.”

Malik felt a sense of pride swell within him. His dad's words reaffirmed his belief in the transformative power of music and the role he had to play in his community. He wanted to be a source of inspiration, encouraging others to embrace their own passions and overcome obstacles.

As the days passed, Malik's music and his message continued to make a mark on community. He organized performances at local community events, sharing his story and the stories of those around him. His lyrics spoke of freedom, of breaking through barriers and embracing individuality. The positive change he aimed to bring was becoming a reality.

Meanwhile, Marcus “LyricalFlow” Johnson remained a guiding light in Malik's journey. The renowned rapper from their neighborhood continued to mentor Malik, offering invaluable insights and support. Marcus understood the importance of staying true to oneself, and he encouraged Malik to explore his unique voice and perspective.

One evening, as Malik and Marcus sat in the basement studio, their voices filled the air with music and wisdom. Marcus leaned back, a satisfied smile on his face. “Malik, you're on the right path, my friend. Your music is not only resonating with people but also bringing them together. It's a powerful gift you have.”

Malik's heart swelled with gratitude. To receive such praise from someone he admired and respected meant the world to him. He looked at Marcus with reverence. “Thank you, Marcus.

Your mentorship has been invaluable to me. I couldn't have come this far without you."

Marcus nodded, his eyes filled with pride. "Remember, Malik, music is not just about entertaining people. It's about telling stories, raising awareness, and sparking conversations. Your voice matters, and I believe in the positive impact you can make."

Their conversation reminded him that his music was not just a form of self-expression but also a tool for social change. He embraced his role in the community, using his music to shed light on issues that mattered and to inspire others to find their own voices.

As the days turned into weeks and the weeks into months, Malik's purpose became clearer than ever. He realized that his music was not only an outlet for his emotions but also a platform to empower others. He sought collaboration with local artists and activists, using his voice to shed light on social injustices and to promote unity and understanding.

In one of their performances, Malik shared the stage with an up-and-coming spoken word artist named Amara. Together, they created a powerful fusion of music and poetry, their words intertwining to create a symphony of hope and self-worth. The audience listened intently, their hearts open to the messages of empowerment and unity.

As the performance came to an end, the crowd erupted in applause. Malik stood on the stage, his heart pounding with a mix of gratitude and excitement. He had found his purpose, and he knew that his journey had only just begun.

In the days that followed, Malik's music continued to touch lives and inspire change. The bonds he had formed within his community grew stronger, and his circle of support expanded. He understood the importance of staying true to himself, embracing his identity, and using his voice to create a positive impact.

Malik's journey of self-discovery and purpose had transcended the boundaries of his own aspirations. He had become a beacon of hope and inspiration for those around him, using the power of music to bridge gaps and initiate meaningful conversations. And unbeknownst to him, his influence and impact had stretched far beyond his neighborhood.

In a serendipitous twist of fate, a video capturing Malik's heartfelt performance of "Rise Above" had gone viral, catapulting him into the spotlight and transforming his life in ways he could have never imagined.

It was a small, intimate performance at a local music venue. Malik poured his heart and soul into his performance, channeling his emotions into every lyric and captivating the audience with his raw talent and infectious energy. Little did he know, a spectator had captured the entire performance on video.

The video captured the essence of Malik's artistry, showcasing his commanding presence, powerful vocals, and the poignant message behind "Rise Above." With its uplifting lyrics and heartfelt delivery, the rap song spoke to people from all walks of life, touching a chord deep within their souls.

As the video spread like wildfire across social media platforms, viewers were moved by Malik's authenticity, his ability to convey a message of hope through his music. The video became a rallying cry, inspiring countless individuals to rise above their own challenges and embrace their true potential.

Within days, the video had amassed millions of views, sparking a wave of support and recognition for Malik's talent. Messages of admiration and encouragement flooded in from all corners of the globe, propelling Malik into the spotlight and igniting a fervor of anticipation for his future musical endeavors.

The viral success of "Rise Above" opened doors of opportunity for Malik. Record labels and music industry professionals took notice, eager to collaborate with this emerging talent. Media outlets clamored to interview him, eager to hear the story behind the young artist who had captured the hearts of millions.

Through it all, Malik remained grounded and focused. He recognized the responsibility that came with his platform and saw it as an opportunity to not only share his music but also to inspire others and advocate for positive change. With grace and humility, he embraced the whirlwind of attention, always mindful of his purpose and the impact his music could have on the world.

The viral success of "Rise Above" not only propelled Malik's career to new heights but also strengthened his resolve to use his voice for meaningful storytelling and social impact. He continued to create music that deeply connected with listeners, forging a powerful bond between artist and audience, addressing important social issues, and offering messages of empowerment, love, and unity.

Beyond the numbers and the fame, the viral video served as a reminder of the power of music to connect, uplift, and inspire. Malik's journey from a talented but undiscovered artist to a viral sensation exemplified the transformative nature of art and its ability to transcend boundaries and touch the hearts of people around the world.

As Malik continued to ride the wave of success, he remained true to himself and the values that had shaped his journey. His rise to stardom was not just about personal achievements but also about the people who had supported him along the way—Travis and Mariah, and the friends, family, and fans who believed in his talent and embraced his message.

With every performance, every interview, and every song, Malik stayed grounded in his purpose, reminding the world that his artistry was more than just a viral moment—it was a testament to the power of a self expression and embracing ones journey, and the universal language of music that has the power to unite, heal, and inspire.

As Malik reflected on his journey, he couldn't help but smile. He had found his voice, and with it, he was determined to amplify the voices of others. The path ahead was filled with challenges, but he knew that as long as he stayed true to himself and followed his dreams, he would continue to make a difference—one lyric, one beat at a time.

Chapter 12: Rhythms of Redemption

alik's journey took yet another unexpected turn that would forever shape his future. It began with a life-changing invitation from none other than Marcus "LyricalFlow" Johnson himself.

When Malik received the call from Marcus, inviting him to join him on the last two days of his tour as a guest performer, he couldn't believe his ears. It was a dream come true, an opportunity to learn from his idol and showcase his talent to a wider audience. Without hesitation, Malik eagerly accepted, knowing that this experience would be a turning point in his musical journey.

The next two days were a whirlwind of excitement, travel, and a surge of inspiration. Malik joined Marcus on the tour bus, embarking on a journey that would take them to cities he had only ever dreamed of visiting. As they traveled, they bonded over their shared love for music, sharing stories, insights, and laughter along the way.

During those intimate moments spent with Marcus, Malik

gleaned invaluable lessons about the music industry, performance techniques, and the art of storytelling through rap. Marcus, always generous with his knowledge and guidance, had became more than just a mentor—he became a friend and a beacon of inspiration ever since their collaboration on the "Anthem."

The backstage preparations, the adrenaline rush before stepping on stage, and the roar of the crowd as Malik took his place alongside Marcus were all moments that would forever be etched in his memory. Together, they delivered powerful performances, their voices intertwining in a symphony of words that resonated with the audience.

As Malik stood on stage, the energy pulsating through his veins, he felt a profound sense of confidence and purpose that he had never experienced before. Marcus' belief in him had ignited a fire within, pushing Malik to new heights and empowering him to explore the depths of his creativity as a lyricist.

Throughout those two days, Malik soaked up every bit of knowledge and wisdom that Marcus shared. He observed the way Marcus commanded the stage, captivating the audience with his words and presence. He witnessed firsthand the impact of music on people's lives, the way it had the power to heal, inspire, and bring communities together.

But it wasn't just the performances and the lessons that left a lasting impact on Malik; it was the genuine connection he formed with Marcus. In those fleeting moments between rehearsals and shows, they had heartfelt conversations, sharing personal stories and dreams. Marcus became a guiding light, reminding Malik of the importance of staying true to himself, following his passion, and never losing sight of the power of his own voice.

As the final notes of their last performance together echoed through the venue, the audience erupted in thunderous applause, their cheers serving as a testament to the impact Malik had made with his music.The tour had come to an end, but the memories, the friendships, and the lessons learned would forever remain imprinted in Malik's heart.

Returning home, Malik carried with him a renewed confidence, a sense of purpose, and an unshakable belief in himself. Marcus' invitation and the experiences shared during those two days had ignited a flame within Malik that would continue to burn bright, guiding him on his path of self-discovery, resilience, and the pursuit of his dreams as a rap artist.

Back at home, and still on a natural high, Malik sat at the kitchen table, his textbooks spread out in front of him, reflecting on his journey and all the changes that had taken place in him and around him and how different he felt about his academics.

The once chaotic space now exuded a sense of calm and focus. His skills as a rapper continued to grow, and with that growth came a newfound self-confidence that spilled over into other areas of his life, school in particular.

Now, as Malik walked the halls of Winston High, a sense of confidence and purpose radiated from him like never before.

The once-familiar hallways now felt like a different world—a world where he belonged, where he had discovered his voice and found recognition as an artist.

Gone were the skeptical glances and judgmental whispers that had once followed him. In their place, admiration and respect filled the air. Students and teachers alike greeted him with smiles, acknowledging his growth and the positive impact he had made. The transformation in Malik's academic performance and his burgeoning success as an artist had not gone unnoticed.

The walls that had once felt confining and oppressive now seemed to burst with inspiration. Bulletin boards showcased posters and articles featuring Malik's performances and achievements. His music resonated through the hallways, as classmates and teachers hummed his catchy hooks and recited his empowering lyrics.

Peers who had previously overlooked Malik now approached him, expressing their admiration and asking for his autograph. He had become a beacon of inspiration, proving that with resilience, self-expression, and a steadfast belief in oneself, anything was possible. The halls of Winston High had become a stage where Malik's talent and passion were celebrated, uplifting the entire school community.

Teachers who had once doubted his potential now sought his perspective and insights during class discussions. Malik's growth had shattered preconceived notions and opened doors for meaningful conversations about identity, creativity, and the power of self-expression. His journey had not only impacted his own life but had sparked a ripple effect, inspiring others to embrace their unique talents and pursue their dreams.

Walking through the halls, Malik was greeted by supportive nods, encouraging words, and genuine connections. The atmosphere was infused with a renewed sense of possibility and a shared belief that everyone had the capacity to rise above their challenges and embrace their true potential.

With each step, Malik felt a deep gratitude for his journey—a journey that had brought him from the depths of self-doubt and academic struggles to a place of self-discovery, resilience, and fulfillment. He had not only found his voice as an artist but had also discovered a community of peers, teachers, and mentors who had rallied behind him, supporting his growth every step of the way.

Malik took a deep breath, and let out a long sigh of relief as the moment of introspection came to an end. Just then, his parents walked in.

They sat with him at the kitchen table, a wave of nostalgia washed over them. Dad broke the silence, his voice filled with pride. "Do you remember when Malik used to struggle in school, Mom? Look at him now—dedicated, focused, and excelling in his studies. I couldn't be prouder."

Mom smiled, her eyes glistening with pride. "Yes, I remember those challenging times. But it's incredible to witness his growth. Music has truly been a catalyst for change in his life."

Malik nodded, appreciating the acknowledgment from his parents. Their support and encouragement had played a significant role in his transformation, and he was grateful for their unwavering belief in him.

Their conversation was interrupted by the sound of the front door opening. Ma, entered the house, her presence carrying a sense of wisdom and serenity. She took a seat at the table, a knowing smile on her face.

"Ah, my talented grandson," Ma said, her voice laced with warmth. "Your music has brought so much joy to our lives. We've had some deep conversations in the past. I've known all along you had the spirit of a poet within you. I hope and pray you take time to enjoy all the good things coming your way."

Malik's heart swelled with love for his grandmother. Her spiritual guidance and support had been a constant presence throughout his journey. She had instilled in him a sense of purpose and connectedness to his roots.

The conversation shifted to Malik's girlfriend, Mariah, who had been pursuing her own aspirations in the fashion industry. Dad leaned forward, a curious expression on his face. "How's Mariah doing with her fashion endeavors? I remember she had big dreams."

Malik's face lit up as he shared Mariah's recent success. "She's doing great, Dad. She got a break in the industry and is now interning with a renowned fashion designer. She's living her dream, and I couldn't be happier for her."

The discussion about Mariah sparked a realization within Malik. Just as he had found his passion and purpose in music, Mariah had discovered hers in fashion. They were both on separate paths, yet intertwined in their shared pursuit of self-expression and creative fulfillment.

J.R., Malik's younger brother, entered the kitchen, his eyes alight with excitement. Inspired by Malik's journey of self-discovery and artistic growth, J.R. had found his own passion ignited. He had always been a video game enthusiast, spending hours playing and exploring virtual worlds. However, with Malik's encouragement and guidance, J.R. had decided to channel his love for gaming into something more.

"Hey, guys!" J.R. exclaimed. "Guess what? I've started a YouTube channel where I create video game tutorials and share my gaming experiences. I want to inspire others to find their passion, just like Malik has inspired me."

Malik couldn't contain his pride for his younger brother. "That's amazing, J.R.! I'm so proud of you for embracing your passion and sharing it with others. Your channel is going to be a huge success."

The room buzzed with excitement and pride. Each member of the family had found their own path of self-expression and fulfillment. The journey of redemption and growth that Malik had embarked upon had rippled outwards, inspiring those closest to him.

As they gathered around the kitchen table, all of a sudden, a familiar tune came through the speakers. "Wait, turn that up!" Malik shouted. "That's my song!"

The room was filled with laughter, joy, and the sweet melodies of Malik's music streaming through the speakers. It was a moment of pure happiness, a celebration of how far Malik had come on his incredible journey of self-discovery.

With his family by his side, Malik's music reverberated throughout the room, infusing it with an undeniable energy and a sense of togetherness. The lyrics of his tracks flowed through the air, connecting their hearts and souls, and serving as a testament to the power of unity and love.

His parents, moved by the transformation they had witnessed in their son, couldn't help but join in the celebration. They danced and swayed to the rhythm, their smiles radiant as they embraced the music that had become an integral part of their lives. It was a moment of pure bliss, a reflection of the unbreakable bond between them.

J.R., Malik's younger brother, eagerly joined the impromptu dance party, showcasing his own moves and sharing in the contagious joy that filled the room. The family's laughter and cheers blended harmoniously with the music, creating a symphony of happiness that echoed through the walls.

As the evening unfolded, Malik's music playing on the popular streaming app became a testament to the power of dreams, determination, and the unwavering support of loved ones. The tracks that once resided only in his heart now uplifted and motivated listeners around the world, touching lives and inspiring others to find their own voices.

In that magical moment, Malik realized that his journey was not just about his personal triumphs, but about the love, connection, and shared experiences that music brought to his family and their community. It was a reminder that music had the extraordinary power to bridge gaps, heal wounds, and create lasting memories.

With the night coming to a close, the family embraced one another, their hearts overflowing with love and gratitude. They knew that their bond had been strengthened through Malik's journey, and they cherished every step they had taken together.

Right then, as the music swirled around them, they understood that their journey was far from over. Together, they would continue to embrace life's challenges, celebrate their triumphs, and make beautiful memories, always connected by the rhythms of love, laughter, and the enduring power of Malik's music.

About the Author

Charles E. Jackson II is a Marine veteran, speaker, and Relational Growth Strategist hailing from the vibrant shores of Daytona Beach, FL. With a passion for inspiring and empowering others, Charles brings his unique perspective and life experiences to the pages of "Rhythm and Resolve: Finding My Voice."

Drawing from life experiences and his personal journey of self-discovery, Charles weaves a captivating narrative that resonates with readers of all backgrounds. As a father and husband, he understands the importance of family bonds and the transformative power of love and support.

Beyond his role as an author, Charles is a seasoned speaker and Relational Growth Strategist, dedicated to helping individuals and organizations unlock their full potential. With a charismatic presence and an innate ability to connect with others, he brings his messages of resilience, purpose, and personal growth to audiences around the world.

Charles's own journey of self-discovery and his passion for empowering others shine through his writing. "Rhythm and Resolve: Finding My Voice" is a testament to his belief in the transformative power of embracing one's true self and the impact of music as a catalyst for personal and collective change.

With his engaging storytelling and inspirational insights, Charles E. Jackson II invites readers to embark on a journey of self-exploration, reminding them that their voices matter and their stories are worth telling.

When Charles is not writing, he enjoys movies and the great outdoors with his wife Zonnette, and sons Jathan and Jaden.

You can connect with me on:
- https://www.linkedin.com/in/charlesjacksonmedia
- https://www.instagram.com/charlesjacksonmedia
- https://www.rhythmandresolvebook.com